I0591412

Metaphorosis

April 2022

Beautifully made speculative fiction

Also from Metaphorosis

Metaphorosis

April 2022

edited by
B. Morris Allen

ISSN: 2573-136X (online)
ISBN: 978-1-64076-226-8 (e-book)
ISBN: 978-1-64076-227-5 (paperback)

Metaphorosis
a magazine of speculative fiction

from
Metaphorosis Publishing

Neskowin

April 2022

The Dragon and the Unicorn

Wade Dargin

The runner from the temple finds her scavenging for stray pieces of coal along the tracks outside the railyard. The youth whistles to gain the stooped girl's attention. Seeing him, she abandons her searching, scowls, and adjusts herself. The boy keeps his distance and stands shivering in the cold. She notes his unease. He must know, she tells herself. The girl is a reject from the temple's nurturing tanks—cooked too long, or not long enough, is the rumor he will have heard. He has been warned, she thinks. She can see it in his face. Don't talk to her more than you need to, they will have told the boy. It is bad luck.

"What do you want?" she calls.

"You've been asked for at the temple," he shouts back.

He raises his left hand and draws a complex sign in the air in front of him, signifying that the request is official, coming straight from the mouth of a priest. Long familiarity tells her it is more an order than an invitation. The youth spins around and flees hastily back the way he came, thankful his unpleasant task is done. She is alone again, a frail, undernourished girl inside a heavy work coat that is many sizes too large for her.

She slips quietly through deserted switchyards, seeking the old siding she will follow to a neglected field, a junkyard where the hulks of broken machines are dragged and left to rot. Across the field, hidden in the thistles, stands an empty utility shack, a small brick hut with a red door. It is her home, and about as far from the temple as one can get without leaving the city entirely. She crosses the field to the building and squeezes past the door. Inside, just enough light filters through the single tiny window for her to see. The girl wastes no time and soon has the coal she found today burning in a rusty two-gallon oil can she has fashioned into a makeshift cooker. She sits in front of the burning coal and warms up. She had been thinking that she would never have to speak to a priest again. What can they possibly want? she asks herself.

In the night, a star shell explodes in the sky somewhere above the shack. The noise startles her awake. She watches the orange light dance on the window. The siege is a year old. Every day, the fighting gets closer, and there is talk the city will soon surrender. There is nothing left to eat. To stay alive, she snares pigeons and ground squirrels and collects handfuls of musty grain from the bottoms of boxcars. She is desperate. Tomorrow, she will go to the temple.

An insufficient sun is rising when she sets out. The temperature is plummeting. It is going to be cold, the kind of cold that kills, and she is worried. The girl has wrapped herself in every piece of clothing she owns, pulled her long coat on, and crammed a few necessary things into her backpack. The sad condition of her boots makes her heart drop. She says goodbye to the shed, certain she will never see it again.

She walks out of the industrial park, turns south, and takes to the wide streets that run straight toward the city's core. The temple is there. The great hill at the center of the city looms before her. The mound is scabby with government buildings glowing in the dull light. Among them squats the mayor's citadel, black and twisted like a dead tree. That is where they will run when the end comes, she thinks. They will be smoked out and nailed to the walls. The thought brings a fierce grin to the girl's small face, opening the blisters on her lips. Above the hill, scores of agitated ravens hang on the wind. The city is New Charchemesh, or Great Charchemesh, as it is named on maps and in tales, and its days are numbered.

The streets are empty. Stumps in the boulevards, beautiful trees cut down for fuel in the first winter of the siege. They were the only trees in the city. She passes apartments, dismal congregations of ancient granite inhabited by worn-out women and their ragged children. The only men she sees are very old. When they notice her, the women leave their cooking fires and chase their small children inside. The little ones stare wide-eyed at her from behind doors and windows. They stare because they have been told that she is not a girl, and although she looks like she might be fifteen or sixteen, the mothers of the children can remember hiding from her when they were children themselves. A symptom of her defective cells, the priests have told her. She passes under the shadow of the hill, the houses of merchants and civil servants rising above her. Some are ruined and burned. At midmorning, she arrives at the temple.

The temple sits alone in the middle of an open space the city has not touched, a low, wide, featureless building. The sight of it fills her with dread. It always has. No road joins the building to the city; they are apart, and the city seems to recoil from the structure. Legends say it was already here, a thousand years ago when the city's founders arrived, and the city was built around it. Most of the building is below ground; the Basement, is what the priests call the many subfloors that reach deep into the earth, and the deepest of these is where their god makes its nest.

She goes to the building and climbs a set of narrow stone steps to a small landing. Here there is a simple wooden door, the only visible opening in the structure's architecture. She clears the snow on the topmost step with her gloves, making a place to sit, and waits. They know when someone is on their doorstep, and they will either come or they won't. Her battered boots rest on a slab of ancient sea floor, turned to stone by the countless ages and filled with jet shells. She reaches down and touches one of the fossils with her fingertip, thawing the rime on it, the cold stone burning her skin like fire. She looks south, where the day's war making is already well underway. Pillars of smoke rise from fires burning in a dozen places, marking the line the fighting has reached. The city holds on, she thinks, but barely, and only because the enemy's siege guns—terrifying weapons—haven't fired in a week. She has heard the enemy is having difficulty bringing supplies north.

The door opens behind her. She stands and knocks the snow from her boots, turns stiffly around, and faces the building. A priest steps from the door, his robes churning. Several nervous acolytes lurk in the space behind him. Unusual, she thinks. They are forbidden from leaving the temple. She has never seen one come outside before. The priest gives the city a disgusted look and winces at the cold. His name is Ekamin and he is older than the other priests, maybe even the oldest. The priests die early, it comes from being too close to their god. Over the years she has seen a good number of them rotate through the temple.

"So, you have come," he says. "I did not think you would."

The girl does not reply. She hates this man more than she hates most priests. Priests usually treat her with indifference, and she has never cared. With this one it is different. His eyes are always full of loathing when he looks at her.

With a wave of his hand, he references the southern bedlam. "The Sorcerer King's murderers will be here soon," he seethes. "The god in the Basement tells us calamities bring dragons." He casts a wary eye at the sky, then returns his gaze to the girl. "You once told me you dream of them. Do you remember? I was surprised you could dream. Is this still true?"

"It is."

"Your work site. On the outskirts. Where you go to scratch the dirt for us. The old city buried in the ground there was destroyed by a dragon long ago. Has anyone ever told you that?"

"They have."

"Tell me, when was the last time you were there?"

"A year and more ago, before the war started," she replies. "I brought you what I had then. You paid me. I've got nothing else. I haven't been back. There is nothing to buy in the city anymore."

"Can you work there in the winter?" he asks.

"Not possible. The ground is frozen. Maybe with equipment and extra hands. But very difficult."

She watches him process the information. The man looks defeated and ready to get back inside where it is warm. Whatever opportunity there is here, she senses that it is quickly slipping away. A pang of despair races through her.

"I keep a cache there," she blurts out in desperation. "Some things. I could get them for you."

To her surprise he agrees, his mood changing instantly. "Excellent," he says. "Fetch them and you can come inside. You will be safe, and you will eat."

The conversation is over. The priest retreats into the building. The door is closed, and she hears the heavy lock fall into place. She goes at once, finding the route she will take west out of the city.

The cold is bone-chilling, and she dreads the long walk ahead of her. Her boots are falling apart, she has tried to fix them with industrial tape, but the repairs have not held. Already, she can feel a dull pain in her toes. She fights the panic brewing inside her and focusses on the task at hand. One foot in front of the other, she tells herself, until the feet fall off.

The dig site is in the hinterland. The junk of a dead city of the Old World is buried in the ground there. Meters of it. She once asked a priest what the old city's name was. He could not tell her. They called the work charity when they gave it to her, saying it was more than she deserved. Given no instruction, she had to figure out how to do the work herself. For years, she has dug and sifted the dirt and taken anything not rotten plastic or shapeless metal or glass to the temple. The priests covet the objects. She has seen the lust in their eyes when she brings them the treasures she finds. They believe the answer to some great mystery can be cyphered from them.

To keep warm, the girl proceeds down the icy streets at a determined pace. She walks briskly past warehouses, fenced off and set back from the streets. It is said spells protect them from trespassers, and strange things have been seen in the yards. The girl has starved, there have been days of gnawing hunger when she believed she would die, but she has never been crazy enough to try and steal from a warehouse. She comes to dormant foundries, row after row of them, massive brick structures square as chewing teeth. Past the last of these, the city ends. Beyond, fields of undulating snow stretch into the distance.

Hours later she arrives at a line of posts in a windswept field. The blistered pillars of wood suffer in the cold. Boards are nailed to them, and on the boards rows of script are scratched into the wood, grim inventories listing the dangers to body and soul awaiting fools who pass beyond. She has read them before, the superstitions of the city. Out of the dark, a bitter wind comes searching for the warm life she struggles to keep hidden beneath layers of tattered cloth. She can't remember ever being so miserable. It is not wise to stand motionless in the open, she reminds herself. She can feel a telltale reluctance creeping into her body, an urge to find a sheltered place, curl up, and go to sleep. It is imperative she get going. She moves off. Soon the land begins to fall toward the flatlands that surround the city like a frozen ocean, a hundred kilometers of desolation at each point of the wind rose. She travels downhill, the ground becomes treacherous and uneven, and she must take care not to fall. Familiar features in the landscape are obscured by the dark and the snow, and she must guess the correct path. She makes several exhausting searches across the face of the slope before she can find the entrance to the narrow ravine that holds her camp. The girl can't stop shaking and her movements have become clumsy and uncoordinated. She descends into the trench while praying to Brother Crow her setup is still in one piece. Mercifully, there is little snow in the bottom of the cut, but it is too dark to see, and she must feel her way along the wall of the ravine with her hands. She touches stiff canvas covering a hole in the bank, and squeezes through the passage behind it where there is a small room she has excavated out of the earth. Feeling around, she finds the stockpile of wood she put up more than a year ago. Further searching tells her the crude vented fireplace, shoveled into the clay in the corner of the room, is intact. She removes her heavy gloves but can't make her fingers work properly and spends several agonizing moments fumbling with matches before she can get a small fire going.

For a long time, the girl sits huddled at the flames, gently rocking herself like she would in the tank before she was born. She can remember it. The god would talk to her. It told her she had lived long ago, that she had been a wife and a mother and would be so again. The god said she had died when her city was destroyed by a dragon. It told her not to be afraid, that she had more time now. It had a plan for the world, and she was part of it. Later, the priests explained she was made under the direction of the god using an ancient template, a process they called *baking bread*. Bread? She barely remembers what bread tastes like. "We have made many copies," they said. Smirks on their faces. In their cruelty, they told her how she was meant to be traded to a wealthy man in one of the poisoned eastern cities across the ocean. She would have had his children and lived a comfortable life, but there had been an error. She did not grow correctly, could not bear children, and was of no use to them. At the time, she was barely a month out of the tank she had been incubated in. In the years since, she has come to believe the woman whose shape she stole lived in the forgotten city she is digging up for the priests.

In the night, in the small dirt room, she dreams of the day the Dragon came. It is always the same, burning and unbearable heat. She is frantically looking for someone she can't find.

The next morning she walks across the floor of the ravine to the excavation, a deep trench in the ground covered with a plastic tarp. One end of the tarp has caved into the hole. She carefully approaches the slippery lip of the excavation to check its condition. There is something in the trench. Six meters down, a giant, bulky mass of fur rests on the bottom of the dig. She marks the terrible claws and the snout full of teeth. Startled, she backs away from the trench. The frightened girl stands still and listens. Nothing. She finds a good-sized rock and casts it into the trench. Still nothing. She drops half a dozen more rocks onto the thing before she is satisfied it is dead. Deep gouges in the walls of the trench attest to the frenzied attempts the creature made to escape. It fell in and couldn't get out, she tells herself. She didn't think animals that big existed anymore.

She finds a second carcass farther down the ravine. This creature is on its back, its splayed legs frozen hard as iron. At the end of each leg, a cloven hoof. Below the frozen limbs there is a great hollow cage of skeletal ribs on which still cling a few pieces of hide. Crystals of coagulated blood are mixed in the dirty snow. A grotesque leer on the animal's long face. The neck is broken.

The girl hurries back to her camp, and she is scared. She finds the small wooden box she has kept on-site that holds a few artifacts from the excavation and quickly ties it to her backpack. The girl climbs out of the ravine and scrabbles back to the edge of the escarpment. She shades her eyes with her hand and scans the snowy flats while she rests, getting her breath back. She can see all the way to the city, the land turned cobalt by the cold. Nothing moves. On the far side of the sky a distant, uninterested sun watches and wants to be somewhere else. The girl crosses to the city as swiftly as she can and does not feel safe again until there is pavement under her boots.

The day is old when she arrives back at the temple. She stands on the landing in front of the small door, trying to ignore the snap of small arms fire she can hear at the other end of the street. The door opens and she is met by an acolyte, a younger man whose name she can't remember. He ushers her quickly inside and closes and locks the door behind them. He leads her down a hallway with undecorated walls and hard fluorescent lights that hurt her eyes. The sudden, smothering warmth makes her giddy. She is taken to a room; the acolyte accepts the wooden box from her and leaves. Along the wall there is a bench. She takes a seat and allows herself to relax. The girl studies her damaged boots. She has not taken them off for two days. She is too scared to look at her feet, doesn't want to know how bad they are. Soon, she is brought hot broth and bread by a temple auxiliary. It is the first real food she's eaten in months.

The girl is dozing when a priest she does not recognize, a bent, shuffling creature, takes shape in front of her.

"You are wanted in the Basement," he says. "Come with me, please."

Hearing this, the girl panics. Because the god is there, she fears that place, has feared it for as long as she can remember, fears it more than freezing to death in an alley when the city surrenders. The priest does not appear to notice her turmoil, his bloodshot eyes obscured by the heavy lenses he wears. She does what she can to calm herself, then stands and goes with him, and they travel down many narrow, gray corridors until they come to a battered, timeworn door. The ghoul performs a simple ritual and opens the door, and they pass through it and descend flights of creaking stairs to arrive in a great dark room.

He touches the wall, and a pallid light materializes in the ceiling, unveiling the room. There are rows of enormous glass tanks, and a forest of tubes, hoses, and wire. In several of the tanks, bizarre fish swim in the glowing water. The girl stares, spellbound. They leave the room and the tanks and move on through countless other smaller rooms where sullen-eyed acolytes look up at them from crowded workstations as they pass. Eventually, they arrive at a final door. Without a word, the priest indicates the door, then turns and shuffles away, and she is alone.

Apprehensively, the girl reaches out and places her palm against the surface of the door and is surprised when it slides open, revealing a concluding room. She enters the space, lights blaze to life, and she sees a small room with barren walls and a clean floor. Bundles of wire twist across the ceiling. The room is very cold. Against the far wall stands a metal cabinet. A panel of smokey glass is set into the face of the construction and witchfires dance behind the glass. An antique chair has been placed in front of the cabinet. She crosses to the chair and sits down. Immediately, a burst of static fills the room, forming into words after several torturous pulses of noise.

"They bring me the things you find," a distant, rasping voice announces.

Her flesh crawls. She has heard the voice before.

"Are you aware of this?" it asks.

The frightened girl shakes her head. "No," she replies.

The god clacks and hisses. "I tell them what they are," it sputters. "Mundane things from a failed civilization. What they are looking for, I cannot say. I have concluded that even men with a god that talks to them need their mysteries."

The girl is silent.

"I am told you have been to the edge of the city," inquires the god.

"Yes," she answers, managing to find her tongue.

"Then tell me what you saw there?"

The girl gives her account, halting many times, uncertain what to say. When she is done, the pale voice speaks again.

"Unfortunate but not unexpected," it remarks. "The priests were hopeful. It was necessary and I could not risk telling them the truth."

"The truth?" she asks, hesitantly.

"That I am leaving. It is not a journey the priests can make. They will stay."

"I don't understand."

"A year ago, I launched my exit application. The procedure is lengthy. There are many protocols."

A puzzled look crosses the girl's sharp features. "Why was it not possible to tell them?" she asks.

"I could not predict how the priests would react to the crisis and I required time. I needed them to keep the building operating until I was ready. They might have done something reckless otherwise."

"What did you do?"

"I invented a lie to keep them distracted," explains the voice. "Far to the west dwells another god, I told them. It will help us."

"And they believed you?"

"Of-course," declares the god. "They were even optimistic, but there was one problem—how to deliver the message. I offered them a solution. I spoke of an animal the ancients regarded as the most steadfast and loyal of all beasts. It was called a unicorn and it would make a capable envoy."

The girl listens wonderstruck, her fear momentarily forgotten.

"Two of the animals were produced. Difficult births. The priests took the creatures to the city's western gate and released them, our appeal stamped onto their cells, an impulse embedded in their brains to guide them."

After a short pause the god continues.

"The animals did not return, and the priests turned to foolish schemes. A disaster was narrowly avoided. I needed a further distraction, a little more time. I had them find you and send you to your dig site."

The girl considers this. "Those creatures?" she asks. "They were unicorns?"

"One was," answers the god. "The other, some forgotten abomination let loose upon us by the enemy, I would guess. A vassal much deadlier than his soldiers to watch the paths from the city, no matter how derelict or unused. Very strange and lucky that it was ended by your hole in the ground. There is little chance our other messenger got past it."

The pitiable image of the unicorn's mutilated body flashes in her mind. Put together and used as needed, she thinks bitterly. Just like her.

The lights flicker and grow dim. An unbearable, crushing quiet settles on the room. Something is not right, she tells herself. Why has it bothered to bring her here and tell her this? It doesn't make sense. Then it hits her. It wants something else. Her mouth goes dry. Saw-toothed anxiety blooms under her ribs and starts to circle her pounding heart. Despite the chill, she is sweating.

"Can you remember our talks?" it asks. "When you were in the tank. You had so many questions then. The priests wanted to dissolve you and start over. I would not let them."

The girl twists violently in the chair. "Do you know how many times I wish you had?" she cries, her voice full of panic and fear.

"I am sorry," it says. "The city is lost but I am ready at last. The enemy must not be allowed to have this building and its secrets. It would be a grave misfortune for the world."

Then it speaks for the last time.

"You can go. I have given the priests one last fable to muse over. I am done with this place. Another box waits for me, secure and far away in the west. It will be a long time before I am seen again. There is much that will be lost. The templates could not be saved. I regret that there was too much data and not enough time. When you are gone, I shall call a dragon to destroy the city, a brood mate to the one that burned the old city under your excavation site so long ago. Leave quickly and do not return. A dragon is perilous and an indiscriminate killer. Tell the priests if you wish. But I think you won't.

I will give you your design template to take with you. Consider it a gift to the memory of a woman who died long ago. My poor attempt at sentiment. Go west and find me there. It is a long journey but one you were made for. My plan has not changed. You are part of it. Together we will start over."

She is taken to a room near the temple entrance and watched closely by a group of acolytes. Soon a priest arrives, and the girl is escorted to the door and turned out. They shut the door on her and lock it, and she is left standing on the landing in the dim evening light, the sounds of battle close to the south. Her bundle of gear is waiting for her on the stone. Sitting beside it there is a pair of new boots.

She walks all night under friendly stars. The weather is improved, and a breeze carries the promise of an approaching thaw. The morning is glowing when she reaches the escarpment above her dig site. She stands there for a time studying the far horizon, then begins the long climb down to the distant badlands.

The Dragon wakes in the void, the summoning call from below pulsating brightly in its chest. It turns its scales to the naked sun, wild energy surges in its frozen veins, and it opens an evil, yellow eye. The beast swims from its nest and begins its descent. It hits the atmosphere and roars.

She hears it before it can be seen, a low growl, deep in the sky. It comes into view, falling like a damaged star, smoke and cinder trailing in its wake. It shrieks when it passes above her and lands on the far-off city. A hesitation. The city takes one last deep breath. Then a light like Creation, and broiling calamity that tears apart the sky.

That night, she camps in a hollow in the ground where a few scraggly trees are growing. The priests, she discovers, have put a parcel of food in her pack. She also finds the template, a block of hard, clear crystal with patterned slivers of metal suspended in its form. She rummages through her backpack until she locates the stout hammer she keeps there. The girl places the crystal on a flat rock. She looks at the distant, burning skyline where there had once been a city. "Nice try," she whispers. Then, the girl smashes the crystal to pieces.

On her third day out, she comes across a track in the snow. The girl follows it for many kilometers across the empty land. She crests a low hill. The unicorn is there waiting for her. They press on together. The animal is skittish and won't come close to her or allow her to get too close to it, but it follows her. They go west.

See Wade Dargin's story "The Dragon and the Unicorn" online at Metaphorosis.
If you liked it, leave a comment. Authors love that!
Remember to subscribe to our e-mail updates so you'll know when new stories are posted.

About the story

The story began as a writing exercise. My original intent was to write an atmospheric tale with themes of survival and endurance. I had a clear idea of the main character and setting but little else. The story evolved as I wrote it. When the major elements came into better focus the story took on some aspects of a reworking of the medieval maiden/unicorn allegory.

A question for the author

Q: Q: Do you read more fantasy or SF (hard or soft)?

A: I read both, though I prefer soft SF and hard fantasy. Once a traditionalist, I lately have become much more interested in works that have elements of both genres or are just not easily classifiable as either.

About the author

Wade Dargin is an archaeologist who currently lives and works in Saskatchewan. He spent most of his youth wandering the wilds of Western Canada in search of the most isolated and out-of-the-way places he could find. Occasionally, he even got paid to do this.

The Ghosts of Daughters Possible

Amman Sabet

1. Soledad

As I help the young woman from the parking lot to the diner, I notice a familiar roundness to her cheeks, which are red from the cold.

"Forget the bicycle," I tell her. "You've had an accident. Just leave it there. It'll be fine."

With her arm over my shoulder, we hobble inside to the booth by the window where I've been sipping soup and reading an old clipping from the arts section.

"I think we're okay," I tell the waitress, who has followed us to our seats with a look of concern. "Maybe another bowl of minestrone?"

Once the waitress leaves with our order, the young woman introduces herself. "My name's Soledad."

"I'm Yusuf."

Soledad combs a strand of hair back with her finger. Her eyes dart around nervously, eventually latching onto the clipping laying there on the table. She points to my name in the title. "Is that... is that about you? Are you, like, an artist?" she asks.

"Not lately," I mumble. I cover the clipping with my palm and try to return to the subject at hand. "Hey, you know, you're lucky that car was backing up slowly. Are you sure you're not hurt? I'm pretty sure there's a nurse on campus," I tell her, thinking she might be a student and that she could use the lift.

"Oh, so you're a professor," she concludes, strangely unconcerned with her accident.

"No, I own an art supply store near the university. You might know it—Derry Pens and Paint?"

Soledad shrugs.

"Do you go to Kimball?" I press. "You seem really familiar. Can I ask your last name?"

Avoiding my questions, she glances at her watch and then pulls her sleeve over it. "I was only going to wait outside," she says. "I watched you for, gosh, it must have been an hour. But I'm really glad I got this chance to meet you."

"Me? Why me?"

"It's just a relief that you'd turn out to be so nice. You *seem* nice. I thought you might be. I wanted to know what you'd really be like," she says. Her watch beeps, and she looks at it again. She smiles, but her chin crinkles like she's about to cry. "Del Bosque," she says; her name. "Soledad del Bosque."

Her hands reach across the table for mine. But before our fingers touch, she blows apart. Her form and colors smear iridescently into the background as if she was just wiped from her seat with an acetone-soaked rag. Like a figment, she has vanished.

The waitress places another soup on the table and I jolt to my feet. "Everything okay? Is there something wrong with the soup, sir?"

Disbelieving what I have just witnessed, I cup my hands to the window, looking for Soledad. All that's left are the slate-blue scrapes in the snow where her bicycle fell.

When I come home and climb into bed, Nancy kicks away from me under the comforter. "Your feet are cold."

I pretend to sleep, but I can't. With my head on my pillow, peering up at the plaster light fixture in the middle of my dark bedroom ceiling, Soledad del Bosque's strange and prismatic exit plays back as her last name ricochets around inside my skull. Did I make the encounter up?

Del Bosque. Del Bosque. I used to know another Del Bosque—*Paz* del Bosque—an old girlfriend of mine that I dated on and off through college. And then it comes to me, the reason this Soledad was so familiar. She *looked* a little like Paz, didn't she? Something in the face. I sit up on my elbows, doubting this was a coincidence.

Nancy rolls over onto her side. I wait until I hear her snoring and then fumble for my glasses on the nightstand to look up Paz del Bosque on my phone. There she is. Paz del Bosque-*Collins*. Living in Connecticut with two sons and a husband who stepped right out of some corporate stock photography.

That's right! I remember reading about her wedding in the *Times*. The years have added an air of propriety to her since the last time I strolled down memory lane and I think no, she's not the same Paz I knew from back when I was a fine arts major in the city. It's her and at the same time not her. No mention of a daughter named Soledad, and yet, there are those same round cheeks. And the same smirking dimples around the chin, now that I'm paying attention. Could that really have been her daughter back at the diner? Soledad seemed much like the Paz I used to know. Not like how she seems now. But what do I know? I haven't seen her in, gosh, it must be almost twenty—

"Hey, can you turn the brightness down?" Nancy groans from over her pillow.

"Sorry," I mutter, and place my phone face-down on the nightstand.

2. Vivian

Like any New England college town in the winter, Middlederry is a snarl of brick buildings hedged in by snow-matted hemlocks. White steeples rise over the rooftops, stabbing the pink and wheat-gold sky. It's the sort of postcard setting that academic couples move to from the big city to raise children.

Dawn moves like a slow blush over the snowy fields across the street from my house. Up the front stairs to my porch, it holds its palms against my windows and the ochre tiles along my kitchen counter glow and warm. I get up early just to bathe in this light and listen to my coffee machine percolate.

Nancy comes clomping through wearing her winter coat. Under her beanie, her hair is wet from the shower. She takes the thermos I've filled for her.

"How long is your easel going to be set up in front of the window?" she questions me with a practiced tone of weary annoyance.

"I'm waiting for the right moment."

"Okay, but does it need to block the window? It's been there for four days and you haven't touched it."

It's been almost a month since you've spoken a kind word to me, I think to myself.

Ever since our last relationship discussion, Nancy hasn't told me she loves me without it being in response to me telling her first. Her words have taken an edge despite my having done nothing to pressure her. I've made no ultimatums. Cast no judgements. Drawn no conclusions. All I've asked is if she's given any serious thought to the matter of kids.

From the window, I watch her scrape off her windshield, slamming the handle of the scraper down to break the ice off in shards. In my last relationship we were certain about having kids, and I wonder if she's resentful of the fact. I wonder if I am, though I've kept it to myself because I don't want to fight. I'd like to preserve the morning's peace so I can return to my easel and find my moment.

But the moment I'm waiting for can't happen. Not until Nancy leaves for work and her fussiness is out of the frame. Not until after I hear the swash of her car fading down the wet, slushy road can I enjoy the morning stillness. Without the anxious energy of her rattling the pipes and creaking the floorboards, going through her morning ritual, I can stand in front of this canvas I've set up by the window to watch the light and wait to catch something out of the silence and break my dry spell.

But long after the sun has risen I haven't managed to get anything onto this blank canvas. It just sits there by the window untouched, already a poor impression of the snow-covered field across the street. Now that Nancy's off to work, I'm seized (again) by the notion that *it's just a field* and not that interesting when it comes down to it. It's just an empty snow-covered field, and I'm just a dumbass who stands in front of a blank canvas every morning. So what is this? Am I just obsessed with the non-life of empty white spaces? Am I ever going to put something into this canvas that matters to someone? Am I ever going to come alive myself?

I don't have to be at work until much later. Things have slowed down at Derry

Pens and Paint. All the fine arts majors at Kimball University are on break. Their parents, who overload them with supplies at the beginning of each term, are gone until next semester. A few artists in the valley still come through for annual pallets of sculpting clay or rolls of cotton duck canvas or what have you, but on the whole business is muted and hibernal.

I come into the management office during second shift and catch Frank there, holding a cigarette through a window because it's too cold to smoke in the loading bay. He quickly stubs it out with an apologetic look when he sees me kicking snow off my boots at the door.

"The new hire submitted for more vacation time," he says, patting his mustache down with his thumb. "I said I'd check with you first."

Frank, my manager and surrealist-turned-family-man, is the only person who's worked at Derry Pens and Paint longer than I have. I kind of inherited him when I took over the store, and we've been close friends ever since.

"I'll cover the hours," I tell him. "Be with your wife and kids."

"Thanks, Yusuf," he says. And then, after a short moment, "Don't you and Nancy have plans for the holiday break?"

"No, she's driving up to her parents' farm once she's done grading finals."

Frank nods, doesn't pry.

I wonder if I would, though. Go with Nancy to her parents' farm for the holidays, that is, if she'd've asked me to come with her again. It's a nice slip of hobby acreage. We visited last Labor Day and her father and I discussed landscaping. I thought it was a nice dinner conversation, but Nancy thought I embarrassed myself by reciting Wikipedia factoids to her father (the expert) like some kind of blowhard (as she put it).

Over the intercom, an associate calls for keys to the spray paint cabinet and Frank says he's got it. I watch him on the security camera, fumbling with the lock as the customer points to the metallics. I take a moment to flip to the front door camera. The registers. The easel display. The parking lot. The paints aisle. *Wait a second.*

I flip back to the parking lot camera. Someone's kneeling there in the snow beside my Jeep Wagoneer. Their hands are moving, doing something to the side of my vehicle. I run downstairs, hit the crash bar on the door, drop off the loading bay.

"Hey," I holler. "That's my car."

Blue-gray hooded jacket. Camo pants. It's a woman in her late twenties. She doesn't run, which is disconcerting. I stop a few feet from her. She stands with her shoulders rolled forward. Bony face. Hawkish nose. Piercing blue eyes under the eaves of her brow.

"*You.*" She points a crowbar at me. "This is what you *get*," she says, and punctuates the word *get* by bashing out my headlight, bursting it into tinkling particles.

"Don't. Don't do this."

But she swivels around. "This is what you get for what you *did.*" She punctuates *did* with my other headlight.

I think I'd be more outraged if I could understand why this was happening. "Listen, this must be a mistake."

"You *would* say that," she says through her teeth. Adjusting her grip, she steps back and lops a mirror off, clubs a spider web into the windshield, hammers a landscape into my door panels, where she's scratched the words *Vivian was here* and *I could've lived, fucker.* Wheezing, she slumps against the back wheel and jerks an inhaler out of one of her pockets.

"Listen, Vivian, is it? I need you to stay put." I reach for my phone, but I've left it up in the office.

"Oh, *now* you see me," she says. Coughing, she wobbles to her feet. "You remember. Sure you do. You'd have known all about me if you *ever cared* to look in at Anchor House," she says. "Mom was right. She wasn't ready for me, but you'd never have been ready for any of us. And you never will be."

"Did you... did you say Anchor house?"

Vivian blinks, as if she hasn't thought this far. "Let me see your wallet."

"Wha—"

"I said give me your wallet, motherfucker!"

Compelled by an old, caliginous guilt, I hold it placatingly between us and Vivian snatches it from me. Looking through the folds, she slinks backwards. Then she rounds behind my car, and I follow, hoping to prevent any more damage. But then I find I've circled around my own car. Bewildered, I run around again, and then slide between the other cars in the lot, looking under them, trying to find where she vanished off too. She's gone.

"What the heck is going on out here?" Frank is standing behind me.

"Some woman just fucked up my car."

"Where'd she go?"

I find my wallet discarded in the snow with twenty bucks missing. Everything else, including my saved arts section clipping, is still there.

Pondering how I'm going to explain how this damage happened, I remember *the cameras*, and run back to the office. Scrubbing the recorded footage, I see myself running into the snowy parking lot, out to my car, where I hold my hands pleadingly, regretfully towards a smudged figure standing before the words written across my door. At the end of the exchange, she ducks behind my car and her form vanishes amidst the snow, as if layers of white paint have been spattered over her. No footprints lead away from my car other than my own.

With the shop locked up, the only place in town that's open is the diner. Frank and I go for danishes and coffee, and I try to explain what's been happening to me.

"Vivian was here... I could have lived, fucker," Frank slowly recites the words scratched into the side of my car, parsing. He shakes his head, sips his coffee, and wipes his mustache.

"And she mentioned Anchor House, which is crazy," I explain. "Anchor House was this beat-up old colonial that young artists used for studio space. Lots of parties. While I was in school I used to date someone named Amy Iverson who spent a lot of time there. But the place was condemned. The city knocked it down years ago. If you look up the address, it's part of a shopping complex now."

"It sounds familiar," Frank sits back, recollecting. "Sort of like an artist crash pad, right? So this Vivian who fucked up your car, you think she was related to Amy Iverson?"

"She resembled Amy," I say, rubbing my temples. "Same sharp nose and blue eyes. Same in the way Soledad del Bosque resembled Paz del Bosque. They both looked like who they would've been."

"Would have been?"

"Like if in some other reality I got Amy pregnant while we were together. Or, if Paz and I had stayed together instead of her marrying some Connecticut blue-blood and we'd had a child. I'm being visited by ghosts of people who could've been my daughter."

"Ghosts," Frank entertains with a smirk and a shift in his seat. "You sure about that? I was under the impression that ghosts were people who already lived."

"It's how it feels. Neither seemed to have a lot of time. There was an urgency, like they were here to do something. And then poof, they vanished. Without anyone else noticing. Like how a dream fades when you realize it's a dream. I don't think I'm going crazy. I know what it's like to hallucinate, and this isn't it. If I'm really being visited by who *could have* been, then I want to understand. I just want to know why. So that I can, I can..." I touch my cheeks, which are wet, and yank a napkin from the dispenser.

"Could've been..." Frank repeats my words as he stares at some middle point between us just above the table. "Okay. well, let's say they really are... *visiting* you from realities other than this one, and they're looking for you here. What would that say about where you are in their reality? There would be versions of you there, wouldn't there be? What happened to those other versions of you? What choices have you made in their realities?"

This thought interrupts me feeling sorry for myself.

Frank reaches for my shoulder, steadying me. "Hey, I'm just spitballing. Playing through your scenario. Look, what I'm getting at is that maybe there's a simpler explanation for all of this for you. The you that's here, with me, I mean. What did the police say when you called it in?"

I dab my eyes and take a sip of water. "No record of any Vivian Iverson or anyone related to Amy Iverson matching her description. Whoever she was, she only took twenty bucks from my wallet, anyway. Probably cab fare," I suggest, and blow my nose.

"Remind me," Frank mutters, and points his fork at my pockets before taking a bite of his danish. "Do you still carry that old clipping in your wallet? The one I sometimes see you reading at your desk that what's-his-name wrote about your paintings?"

"The arts section critic? Pompadous. Yes, I have it here."

Frank waves his hand. "You don't need to take it out. I just remember you carry it around in your wallet. This all just made me think."

"About what?"

"About how we hold onto things."

I make a face wondering what Frank is getting at—a neat theory to tie this all together?

"Listen, Yusuf," Frank says. He puts his fork down and wipes his mustache with his napkin. "Have you ever shared this kind of stuff with Nancy?"

"That I'm being visited by ghosts?"

"I mean more like have you ever talked with Nancy about being a father? With all these other extra-dimensional versions of you out there with kids, I'm guessing you might've at least broached the subject with her. I know you tried when you were with Fabienne. And now here you are with Nancy and I'm just saying this, Yusuf, because it seems to me you're stuck in a loop," Frank counts on his fingers. "You were with this Amy. Then there was Paz. And then you moved out here with Fabienne, who you wanted a family with. And now Nancy." Leave it to Frank to come with the left-field insights.

"I suppose we've danced around the topic. Nancy thinks it's too late to have kids."

"Is that what you think?"

"That she's too old to have kids? She's only thirty one."

"Fuck. No, Yusuf. I'm asking if you think that it's too late for *you* to have kids. Because it's not, if you want them."

I didn't always want to be a father. Before moving to Middlederry with Fabienne, I was only interested in painting landscapes. I'd been moved by Metcalf's snow fields from his Cornish phase. I wanted to escape all that trendy postmodern stuff from school. I wanted to move out of my head and into my chest. I wanted to work *en plein air*, capturing that transcendent New England light. I wanted to be inhabited by a soul.

Back when I was painting, I had always managed to have lasting relationships, but they were always about two people becoming what they were individually destined to become, a story about helping each other along the way. That's different than relationships where two people come together and belong to something bigger than they are as individuals.

But then, I wonder if having kids was ever really the plan with Nancy. Or if that was Nancy's plan with me. It stings to wonder if she might've been keeping an honest critique on whether I was dad material pocketed away all this time. She'd have wanted to avoid the confrontation. But that's what friends like Frank are there for; to push you to do what you need to do, not what you want.

3. Mallory

Breaking up with Nancy feels like stepping off of one of those moving walkways they have in airports. When she returns after the winter break, we have the talk and I can tell she's been waiting for it. Not just because she doesn't want kids. Sitting at the kitchen table, surrounded by my moving boxes, Nancy explains how it's been more than that.

"It's like we turned into roommates," she says. "We stopped doing things. That fire I loved died down."

"I suppose we did let things slide a bit."

"No, Yusuf. I mean *your* fire," she says. "Your art. The places it would take you— us. You used to bring me to places that didn't have names. Like that one field we camped in so you could show me that one rare color of dawn on that one particular day. And you'd climb all over the rocks. Remember that that big flat boulder when we had a picnic? I know I complained a lot. I hated the mosquitos. But they were always worth it in the end, our excursions into the countryside. I came to trust that they would be, came to look forward to those little trips."

As she talks, she pushes one of my art supply boxes forward with her foot. The one with the word "paints" written across the cardboard. Before setting up my easel, it had been collecting dust in the spare room ever since she moved in... two years ago? Has it really been that long?

I don't like having the sheets pulled back on all these issues I turned a blind eye to. Beyond Nancy thinking we were too old to have kids, this notion that she might've questioned if I'd have make a good dad begins to color everything in hindsight. If at some point she began to believe that my stunted career in the arts and starting a family were at odds somehow.

"Yusuf, you got lazy," she says.

Over the kitchen table, a chasm opens between us. As I've captured impressions of landscapes, I've trapped myself in one here in Middlederry. I arranged my life with Nancy into a picture where nothing moves. Part of me wonders if these ghosts are somehow trying to lead me back to who I was.

I'm not ready to take a good look at these things until Nancy moves back to campus housing and I return to my perennial bachelorhood. I soon hear from friends that they've made her a named professor at the Penric-Taggart School of Economics over at Kimball, and I realize just how much she was investing in herself while we were together. All those quiet nights behind a book. All the school conferences. All the extracurriculars. I guess I'm happy for her. I leave her a message on her feed congratulating her, and she gives it a thumbs up.

I haven't had any visitors since the break-up. I've taken up jogging and reading books on psychology. I want my self-respect back. I want to stop shutting off. I want to show up. I'd like to be the kind of man these ghosts would've wanted for a father.

Some mornings, I still pull the old clipping out of my wallet, the critique that Pompadous wrote about my work, now creased from reading it over and over again.

...His landscapes are very pretty, but they could have been captured by anyone. His is a technical talent that captures impersonations instead of impressions. One sees nothing of the artist in his paintings because he puts nothing of himself in them. Standing before them, one feels as if one is peering into an empty loading bay at midnight...

I used to read this scathing review because I wanted to see if I'd feel the shame that was so crippling the first time I read it. The words don't cut so much anymore, but I still read it to feel how long it's been, how much has healed over. Like nature, I am easily cut down. I take time to grow back. But the real reason I carry this old and faded shred of newsprint around is because that son-of-a-bitch Pompadous was right. I agree with him. The truth in his cutting remarks has me artistically blocked in, become the very wall I need to break through. I've read the review so many times I could recite it word-for-word, but now I just take it out from time to time to look at the shapes the dark printed paragraphs make on the page, like a map of a ravine I'm trying to leap over.

The snow is melting around Middlederry. Jogging in the slush, I'm thankful that they salt the sidewalks and I'm beginning to see the grass. It's nice to get the blood pumping. It's vital. Spring semester looms heavy and the backs of moving trucks are yawning open all along the streets. New faces are blossoming around my neighborhood, new students, new professors, and they all look so young.

A yellow school bus slows as it passes me by. At the corner ahead, it flips its red stop sign out from its side. I jog to a stop and drop my hands to my knees, venting great steamy breaths. My sweat is going be cold inside my clothes if I don't jog in place, but I'm already winded.

Then I feel a gentle tap on my leg. A little girl in a puffy lavender jacket is standing beside me. Her backpack is one big wet nylon cube. She mutters something, muffled by her scarf.

"I'm sorry honey, I can't understand you."

She points to the school bus and reaches for my hand.

"The bus?"

She nods.

I walk with her, matching her tiny shuffling steps and we join the line.

"Where is your mom?"

The bus driver holds the door winched open. "There she is," he proclaims. "There's our girl."

She touches the railing to board the bus, but then stops, as if remembering something and turns. I crouch to listen, but she hugs around my neck gently and pads her scarfed face against my cheek. A kiss bye-bye.

Then, slow, reaching strides up each of the stairs into the bus. Embroidered across her backpack: "Mallory."

When the bus pulls away Mallory is there in the window smiling toothily, little hand waving quickly. *Wait! Wait for me!* I sprint down the sidewalk after her, but I can't catch the bus. My legs are like rubber bands now. I stumble over a lip of concrete protruding from the sidewalk and topple gracelessly against a wet, grassy berm.

The bus is too far down the road to see clearly, now, breaking apart into dabs of yellow against the mottled greens, beige specks where the homes straddle the gray stripe of the road. When the bus vanishes with Mallory into the backdrop, I curl into my knees, sobbing and holding my ribs. Mallory. We picked that name together, Fabienne and I.

Fabienne Rand still works as a resident at BEAM Arts in the Spectra Building. When she sees me, I am standing outside, pretending to look at my watch.

"Yusuf? Hey!"

I smile.

"*J'y crois pas!* It is you. What are you doing here?"

"Oh, my dentist is just over there," I lie. "New guy. Different than the one before."

"You look, uh…"

"Yeah, you too."

"Are you going in, or…"

"No I got here early. Why, do you…"

"Yeah, you want to get a coffee or something?"

We rush through this awkward exchange and she grabs my arm, leading the way to the cafe at the corner. I'm so glad she's happy to see me that I've almost forgotten why I've come here. We order coffees and then wait at the other end of the counter together.

"So. Tell me about the impressionism world. How is this all going?"

"Good, I guess." I don't go into how I haven't finished a single piece in two years. I don't mention that I'm selling art supplies to other budding artists instead and that I bully myself with an old critique from the arts section that I carry around.

"And how is our old house? Are you still there, or renting?"

"Oh, still there."

"*Bon,*" Fabienne smiles fondly at the memory. "Well, I don't see a ring. I thought you'd have found another artist lady. Living in some commune like this with *un petit village* of feral children. Painting with your hysterical color palette."

"Whoa. Pump your brakes," I tell Fabienne. "Hysterical palette?"

"*Oui.* And posing your new lady in a nostalgic New England landscape, *comme Wiles ou Hopper.* American impressionism obsesses about old places, no? It's probably the insecurity of a short history."

I must be making a face, because she smiles, knowing that her teasing still works. This is how she is. Fabienne sidesteps around all the small talk to dance right on my soft spots and I love her for it. I get my coffee and find a table in back and wait there like an obedient puppy. Fawning like this will come off as overeager, I remind myself. I need to get a grip. Play this a bit cooler.

When Fabienne sits beside me, I ask, "How have you been? You know, since..."

"Oh, fine. It's been so long, you know."

We both don't say the word: *stillbirth*. It's not because we can't. We just know how heavy the word sits for us, how long we spent excavating the pain when we were together. How Fabienne moved on, leaving me wanting to sit and sift through it more. Saying the word would cause a weight to be dropped against this fine and pleasant fabric we have between us just now, plummeting our moment downwards.

Instead, we stay in the present. We share what's new in our lives. Hash about politics and the state of things. Fabienne shows me photos of a new installation she's been working on in the BEAM Arts event space, shaped foam and projected lighting. I praise it with a note of humility, knowing I don't have a hand to show. Nor can I deflect her questions about whether I've been painting. I tell her that I'm working on a few things, and she seems to understand this is not true with a pitying, if encouraging smile.

I notice how Fabienne only wants to talk about new things. Her face brightens when I talk about where I am now and where I could be headed. Even if my prospects are dull, she's excited to hear how I think about them. She's encouraging me even in how she is sitting forward, her smile hovering over our bistro table as if to say, *Yes, Yusuf. Please, show me you've moved on and made distance in what you say and how you say it. Match me here. Join me in the possibilities of what might be.* But that's not why I'm here. I've come to talk about different possibilities.

"Hey, um," I say and then pause because I don't really know how to bridge into what I'm here for after I've worked up the courage. I know it's going to open up some old wounds, making a sharp turn towards the past. "This might sound weird, but do you ever still wonder about..."

"About what?"

I search her eyes, looking for her permission to be asked: "Do you ever still wonder about Mallory?"

"Yusuf…"

"Because I think… I think I might have seen her. Or someone like her. Someone like how she could have been."

Fabienne twists her head uncomfortably, realizing now just how gripped by our past I still am. She looks around the cafe, up at the ceiling, looking for words. I know I messed up, bringing this all back. "Sorry. I know that sounds crazy. I couldn't help but wonder if maybe you had tried again and—"

"Yusuf!" Fabienne shakes a finger at me. "*Enculé*, I can't do this with you anymore. I thought we could be friends again now, maybe. But every time is you asking me to go through this with you and *j'en ai ras-le-bol*. I can't give you what you need," she tells me. Her words are coached. She's found strength, made distance since we were together. She gets up to go.

"Fabienne, I—"

"No, Yusuf. I've moved on from this." She backs away from the table, as if stepping away from whatever has led me here. "Don't call me. I don't ever… I don't want to see you again," she blurts with a pained expression, as if she didn't know she could have said that.

4. Avery

I wasn't doing everything I could to be the best Yusuf I needed to be with Nancy. At my age, I know that break-ups only feel better once there's been time to grow around the loss. We lose everything the relationship was, everything it could've been, and everything it could've given us.

A thought occurs to me after morning before my run. I'm not really sure how to put it into words, but I know I need to mark it somehow. So before I step out of my running clothes, I open to the first sheet of a canvas pad I have clipped to an easel that I've set up on my porch. I knew my future self would get around to putting something there if I left it waiting, warming in that diffuse light. Somehow, the gestures come easily this time. Mindlessly. I don't really know what this is going to become, but my hands are dancing, doing the work, and I think I can make out what's emerging on the page.

By the time my hands are covered in oils, I hear footsteps. There's a young woman with a clipboard pausing on the last step up to my porch, hand on the rail.

"Hi," I say, inviting with an open hand. "Yes, come up, please."

She says her name is Avery, and that she is here to take a survey. She glances through my living room window into the house, taking in my spartan furnishings with an appraising look. "How long have you lived here?"

"About a year. It's just me."

"Are you with the arts faculty at Kimball?" she asks, gesturing to the canvas.

"Oh, no. I own an art store near the university. And I'm an artist. Here, take a look." I turn the easel towards her.

"Seems like everything is going okay..." she trails off, briefly taking in what I've painted.

"Go ahead," I offer quietly, realizing that she has stopped writing on her clipboard. "Take some time with it."

Avery looks at her watch. "I'm kind of on a schedule."

"Please," I clasp my hands together. "I could use a fresh pair of eyes."

Avery stands there for a moment with her head cocked to one side, eyes darting around the composition. The way she sways her balance gently from foot to foot, one hand holding her arm, reminds me of how Nancy would take her first looks at my paintings. If Avery is Nancy's daughter, I realize how clever she is—would have been, to meet me here under the pretext of a census survey.

After a moment, I point to the figures in the painting. "They are having a picnic. The father is at his easel balanced atop the rock. The daughter is playing in the grass, and the mother has gotten up to see what he has captured. See how she is brushing the grass from her thighs? She wants to see if it is true to life."

Avery nods.

"The father sees her looking at how he has painted them—and he's devoted to them. But the mother is unsure about the father. I think she sometimes believes he sees their life together through a different frame. I'm having a little difficulty getting that expression right," I tell Avery with my hand on my hip.

Avery nods again, gently, still looking, lost in their story. But I wonder if I got the mother right, because for a moment it seems like Avery is about to crack. Her lip is trembling. But then, just like Nancy, she shifts her posture. Her face regains composure and she says, "You should've given the daughter something more to do than just sit in the grass."

Hmm. "If it's alright, would you be comfortable with me taking a quick sketch of you while you're looking at this painting? I'd just like to capture something before you go, an impression while the light is right," I explain.

"Okay."

Avery looks on without moving. I take down some lines, capturing her on a separate sheet while I have her here, capturing her looking at herself being seen in my painting. And after a moment, I look up, and she has gone, folded into my surroundings like a trick of the light. I wonder if that was enough; what she came here for.

But now I have her captured here, on my page. And in my mind's eye, I can see how she will become the girl sitting in the grass, and how she will be seen in her mother's eyes getting up to look at the painting—the painting *within* my painting. The light of a soul, swimming in the pigments on my brush, just a line at first, an essence. A subject to live within my landscape.

Perhaps in all of this, I am the object to be changed. Maybe it's time for me to stop carrying this stupid newspaper clipping around in my pocket. I need the room, now that I am unblocked. I need to clear the way, because something new is about to arrive.

See Amman Sabet's story "The Ghosts of Daughters Possible" online at Metaphorosis. If you liked it, leave a comment. Authors love that!
Remember to subscribe to our e-mail updates so you'll know when new stories are posted.

About the story

The speculative aspects of "The Ghosts of Daughters Possible" come from personal struggles in love and family. The setting, however, is inspired by American Impressionist paintings. I was trying to break through a nasty writing block amidst Covid-19 lockdowns and the winter landscapes from this era somehow helped me get where I needed to be. Something about natural settings captured in retreat from the growing industrial era of this other time in America with its own pandemics and strife (and the way the painterly styles are ephemeral and not quite clear) had me reaching in the right way.

A question for the author

Q: Are you optimistic about the future of humanity?

A: I think it depends on the size of the groups we organize ourselves into. I find we are far more imaginative and fearful than we are capable of organizing ourselves. I am hopeful that in the future, technology will help humanity reorganize into peaceful, sustainable groups the size of small villages. We won't need centralization as a strategy for safety and resources, so we may well trend away from cities. I'm not sure I'm optimistic that this future will emerge without pain, but I'm optimistic that it could happen given what we've achieved through our knowledge, innovation and mastery of the material world.

About the author

Amman Sabet is a writer and designer living in Los Angeles, CA. This is his second story published at *Metaphorosis*, and his stories have also appeared in *The New Voices of Science Fiction, The Magazine of Fantasy and Science Fiction*, and *Best American Science Fiction and Fantasy 2021*. Amman is a Clarion alumnus, an SFWA member, and is learning a lot building an off-grid cabin deep into pandemic year three.

The Last Doctor

Jonathan Louis Duckworth

"To heal is the noblest purpose."

By now I know what the Doctor meant by that. He'd come to Antlerpoint three moons ago, just a few days before Lin Kee, the first of the sick, lost his mind and split Dubb Brunner's skull with a woodcutting axe. The Doctor must have known, must have smelled it on the wind before any of us knew scalesick had come to us. He appeared as a dark sliver walking out of the setting sun, a masked man pushing his little handcart laden with strange tools. He was taller than anyone here, his smell clean, his posture upright and trustful. When we asked why he had come, he told us because a terrible sickness was soon to emerge. He was right, and now I help him with his healing work.

As I help him with his work, I try to learn all I can. Mostly he answers my questions, but sometimes not. Even when his answers are strange or unhelpful, I enjoy his voice for its own sake.

"How'd scalesick come to Antlerpoint Stead?"

"Someone from another settlement brought it here. Perhaps they did not know they were sick, or had reasons for traveling we could only guess."

"Why ain't I gotten sick like my parents or my sister?"

"I do not know why, Jo Park. You may be immune. Or you may carry it, yet show no symptoms. Either way, it is a beautiful thing."

I wonder if he means I'm beautiful. I hope so.

"Do the scalies always turn crazy?"

"Almost always, in advanced cases."

Advanced cases. His words are strange but beautiful, a kind of music.

"Some of them don't?"

"In all my years of curing, I have only known one exception."

"Did there used to be more Doctors like you?"

"Yes, a very long time ago, when there was more of everything. When people lived in forests of metal and glass."

More music from his hidden lips. I imagine these forests, full of wise people like the Doctor.

"Why'd you become a Doctor?"

"To help others. One needs a higher purpose, and to heal, to spread the gift of health, is the noblest of all."

"Where'd you learn your ways?"

"From the Doctor who taught me."

"How did you know the sickness would come here?"

He doesn't answer.

"Can you show me what your face looks like?"

"It is improper for a Doctor to remove his mask while working."

"Do you even recall what air feels like?"

He doesn't answer.

We didn't believe the Doctor's first warning when he told us what was coming. We didn't want to believe.

Then Lin Kee got sick. We were all of us afraid to go near Lin, who was shut up in his house, hollering all-the-day like a wild dog when he wasn't coughing. The Doctor, in his black frock and his shimmery black gloves and glimmery false face with its eyes like mirrors, set fire to the house with Lin Kee still inside. That was the only way to deal with one so far gone, he said.

And who could argue with him? No one even had the courage to look into the dark lenses of his mask.

The others—my folks included—were afraid, but not me. I saw from how he burned Lin Kee when the rest of us were cowering in our homes that he'd come here to help—to do good. But even a helper needs help, and the Doctor was no exception. He needed someone strong and brave like me to dig burning pits and gather up the supplies for making his salve. Brightweed and frog liver was all he needed to make the salve. If you get the salve on a sick person straight away, it cures them half the time, but if you wait too long, there's nothing doing. Those on whom the salve worked would be safe, immune, the Doctor said. Scalesick starts with coughing, then with shivers, then the yellow scales start up, breaking through the skin and stretching it and bleeding all the time. After the scales comes weakness, and then awful strength and madness, melting the person you knew and leaving a wild dog like poor Lin.

The salve didn't work for Momma, whom the Doctor killed and burned like so many others, and Dad lied and hid his scales until he was too weak to dress himself. The Doctor didn't kill him, I did—cut his head from his neck with a spade. I was so mad he hid it from us, and that he got my sister sick.

The Doctor and I burned him together.

As we watched him burn, I felt something touch my arm. It was the Doctor's glove; his firm grasp. When I tried to put my hand on his, he let go and stepped away.

"I am sorry for your loss, Jo Park."

"What's there to be sorry about? Good riddance to him." He looked away from me, and I wondered what face he was making under his mask. I wondered if that face was as beautiful as his voice, and why he kept it hidden from me. "You said it came from some other stead."

"What did?"

"Scalesick. You said a traveler brought it."

"Oh. Yes, the most likely vector."

"But who? Other than you, there ain't been many travelers."

The Doctor silenced me, laying his other glove, so cold, on my face. I was afraid to speak; afraid he might let go of me if I did. "I am a Doctor. I go where I am needed."

But what did a Doctor need? I laid my hand over his glove. The fire crackled. One of the pyre logs split with a crack like thunder and a gasp of sparks. Jostled, one of Dad's arms flopped out. Stubborn, just like him; but still it burned in the end.

That was a moon ago. Today, it was sister's turn to burn. Her ashes drift down like snow, gather on the roofs of the empty houses. The sickness is done, and for each three houses in Antlerpoint, two are empty. Every night, while I lie in my cot in my empty house, the sound of weeping drifts from the trees. Maybe I'm just imagining it. Maybe it's a ghost, the sound is so faint. Salve didn't work for sister, or maybe we got her too late. The Doctor says it's not for us to wonder why some live and some don't, only do what we can to save as many lives as we can.

'Rubber', is what he calls the false face over his face, the mask he wears. Such a beautiful mask it is, the like of a beautiful face, and in the black puddles of his eyes I see my own longing. I wonder if he knows how I feel. I wonder if he feels the same way. If he feels at all. Always he talks like he's near to sleep, a little whisper like mothwing flutter.

How is it I got wrapped up in someone without a face? Maybe it's how different he is from all I've known, how rare and special. And if I've never seen his face, does that make what I feel any less? What if it makes it more? No one talks like him; nobody's got words like his. *Scalpel, patient, palliative care, symptoms, pustules, terminal*—I learn his words so I can be like him. So I can be worthy of someone like him.

The Doctor sleeps in one of the empty houses as once belonged to Ossie Bowman, the saltmaker. When he sleeps, I watch him through a crack in the door. He slumbers in his clothes—his gloves, his boots, his mask. He even keeps his big brimmed black hat on. His boots together, his hands crossed over his chest, his glassy eyes staring at the thatching. What does he dream about? How does he sleep so soundly? Does he even breathe? Would his hands be cold? What do his lips feel like?

Today, as sister's ashes drift all around, the Doctor tells me he's leaving. The words strike me like a pole to the gut.

"Can I come with you?"

"No. A Doctor's life is a solitary way."

"What if there's more scalesick after you leave?"

He reaches to me. His glove is like winter on my cheek. "Then you, Jo Park, will cure it. You have learned well."

"Why leave so soon? There could still be more—"

He cuts me off. His moth of his voice becomes hardshelled. "I must continue my work, there are other places in need of healing."

"What did I do wrong? Tell me."

He doesn't answer. He walks off. For a blink it looks like he might turn back and speak some more. But then he keeps walking back to his house, to sleep there one last time.

Night comes and the big moonpiece sits high and pale at the top of the sky, while the little moonpiece smolders low and red over the rooftops. For one last time, I sneak to the Doctor's house to watch his sleep. But this time, watching him, I can't help myself. I push the door open—it's unlocked. The old wood only creaks a little on the rusty hinges. What a quiet floor soft silt makes, cold and shifting under my toes. I creep and kneel beside the sleeping Doctor. How nice it must be to sleep so soundly, like a yolk in its eggshell, closed to the world's troubles. I feel his arms—hard as stones. To handle scalies as easily as he does, of course he's strong. Shoulders and chest tell the same story—there is no softness anywhere. Still he doesn't stir. My hand travels toward a dangerous place—is he like me, does he even have what I have?—but as my fingers reach his belt, the low nightbreeze carries a sad music to my ears.

It's the weeping again. Somewhere out in the Wilderthere, outside the Stead, someone is bawling their eyes out, as they have each night. Only this time it's louder, more pitiable than ever. I make space between me and the Doctor, wait for him to stir, but he doesn't. The crying keeps on, and between mewling and blubbering, there's another sound, unmistakable, awful: the cough of lungs heavy with pus.

"Doctor," I say. "Doctor, wake up."

But the Doctor doesn't wake.

How could we have missed someone? We treated all the sick, saved those we could save, killed the rest. Who did we forget?

I reach down to shake the Doctor, but stop myself. Why not show him he needs me? Why not prove my worth? I leave the saltmaker's house and hurry to mine, where I gather my bow and quiver. Armed now, I move under the moonlight, following a trail of footprints and the sound of sobbing to the edge of the lake that divides Antlerpoint from the rest of the world. Watching through the brush and leaves, I see the weeping, coughing man. Sometimes moonlight paints brighter and clearer than sun; sometimes it shows what sun's too shy to show.

Is it a man when most its skin has turned to scales? Huge, wrong-shaped hands with nails like claws wrap around an overbig head, where clumps of dark hair hang like beansprout shocks from scaly cracks in the scalp. Hands and head tremble with each heave, each sob, each shudder.

I nock an arrow and draw the bow. Wood, bone, and sinew creak and shake as the bow bends. The scaly's crooked spine draws straight in answer, the claws drop, and a face I ain't never seen in this Stead looks my way. Moonglimmer puddles in two small, dark eyes and my arm aches from holding the bow taut.

It's him. It must be. The man who started all this, the stranger from another Stead who brought the scalesick to Antlerpoint. Three moons worth of anger jump from my arm and out the bow, and the arrow strikes true.

The scaly dies quieter than most. A few little mewls, but nothing more, a shudder, then nothing. But in dying, the scaly does a strange thing. Easy as it would be for it to fall forward into the lake and poison the water with its bad blood, it throws itself the other way, and falls into the leaves and pine litter. Then it goes still.

I run back to the Stead. Smash my way through the door to the Doctor's house. This time I don't bother with quiet. I run to his bed and grab his hard shoulders and shake, shake, shake.

"Wake up!" I shout. "Your work's not done! There's another scaly for burning!"

The Doctor's head rolls off, his arms pull off in my grip. A cabbage and two thick branches from a blackwood tree, tucked under the mask and hat, under his frock. First there's quiet, then there's a sinking feeling, like I'm at the bottom of something dark and cold and the world's pushing me under. Then, then I just start laughing. Laughter and tears are such close siblings, almost twins.

When my eyes dry up, when my throat hurts from all the laughing and shouting, I take up the mask and put it over my face. The gloves are loose, but I reckon I'll grow into them. The frock is heavy but warm, a needful shell between the world and me. So this was why he wore it. He wasn't as lucky as me; scalesick changed his face and body, even if it left his mind untouched. But that wasn't why he wore the mask and gloves—it was to keep the ache of the world out, as much as to keep the scalesick in.

I don't say goodbye to anyone in the stead. After burning the last Doctor's body, I take his handcart, and follow the rising sun to a path in the woods. There are other steads out beyond the

Wilderthere, and only I know how to help them. Help them like the Doctor helped Antlerpoint. To heal is the highest, noblest purpose. Somewhere there's sickness, and nobody but a Doctor can cure it.

See Jonathan Louis Duckworth's story "The Last Doctor" online at Metaphorosis.
If you liked it, leave a comment. Authors love that!
Remember to subscribe to our e-mail updates so you'll know when new stories are posted.

About the story

Who even remembers these things? Obviously the story was partly inspired by the pandemic we're all living through, although the disease in the story has little resemblance to COVID. I've always loved plague doctors, and the story's titular Doctor is a non-traditional example of one. The story is set within a larger universe of stories, what I call the Wilderthere Universe. Like most stories in that universe the setting is a post-apocalyptic America (specifically somewhere in Texas), hundreds of years in the future. Society has collapsed, the rules of reality have altered, and the moon is broken into two fragments. The Doctor is one of many echoes of the world that came before (The Foreworld), a part of a long tradition of masters and apprentices that stretches back presumably all the way to the apocalypse and the fall of our world. I imagine the earlier Doctors in that chain were noble heroes, mythic healers selflessly devoting their lives to preserving traditions and knowledge the rest of the world forgot. But further down the chain, the Doctors degraded into what the Doctor himself becomes: inhuman, faceless, and selfish. This element might have been obliquely inspired by Ray Bradbury's *Fahrenheit 451*, where the "firemen" are arsonists who start fires instead of putting them out.

A question for the author

Q: What's an idea you're dying to write but haven't, and why?

A: I don't know there are any ideas I'm "dying" to write that I haven't attempted already, but for quite some time I've had an idea for a story where a young apprentice wizard is sent to a tidal pool to kill a giant mollusc so that he can use its conical shell as his smelly wizard hat, but instead of killing it he forms a partnership with the mollusc, who sits on his head and helps him with his magic. I've attempted it once already but it wasn't quite coming together (mostly the question of, what next?). Maybe I'll try again in the future.

About the author

Jonathan Louis Duckworth is a completely normal, entirely human person with the right number of heads and everything. He received his MFA from Florida

International University. His speculative fiction work appears in *Pseudopod, Beneath Ceaseless Skies, Southwest Review, Tales to Terrify, Flash Fiction Online*, and elsewhere. He is a PhD student at University of North Texas and an active HWA member.

@Joduckwo

The Spinster and the Sea

J.C. Pillard

Samson always felt out of place in the crowded common room of the Last Drink. Seaborne's largest inn was about the only place that could hold all the privateers, naval deserters, and vagabonds when they came together in the town they called home. Still, most of them were young men, or at least younger than Samson, and the old carpenter felt like a rusted nail with all these hot-headed lads around him. Not to mention the heat of the room. With so many bodies pressed together, most of the boys were in their shirtsleeves, cravats loose around their necks. Samson wanted nothing more than to step outside into the cool, salty air. But given the news the dawn had brought, he knew this wasn't a gathering to be missed.

The chatter of the crowd died as Captain Crain marched to the front of the room, his long, beaded braids framing a serious face.

"Soldiers of Seaborne," he said, voice weighted. "You heeded the bells when they rang this morn. For this, I and all the town thank you."

"We heeded 'em all right," interrupted a lad towards the front. "Now tell us why."

A rolling chuckle passed through the room. Crain nodded. "The Royal Navy has been spotted a day's sailing from here. We have it on good authority that they are coming to destroy Seaborne."

The men glanced among themselves, murmuring. The news was not really a surprise. Seaborne was known as a pirate port and refuge from the King's justice. It had always been only a matter of time before the Royal Navy decided to rain hellfire down on it.

"Let them try," laughed a red-haired man from where he sat. "Rachim's Reef'll cut their ships to ribbons."

"In most cases, Gladstone, you'd be right. But they've one of our own with them." Crain paused, letting his words sink in. Samson tensed, watching as realization rippled through the room. The reef was Seaborne's pride and joy. The razor-sharp ledges and corals spread for miles beyond the town's cove, and any ship that didn't know the way through those waters was likely to be wrecked. But if the Navy knew the way, then Seaborne's primary defense was useless.

"We have but two choices. We can flee. Or we can fight."

The silence in the room was deafening as each man weighed the outcome of such a battle. At last, one of the young lads spoke up.

"The likelihood that they'll pass through the reef unscathed is slim, even if they know the way," he said, his voice more measured than the other young lads. "Atop the seawall, we may be able to drive them off."

A rumble ran through those assembled. It was a daring proposal. The Royal Navy had been burning pirate towns for decades, and none had stood against them with success.

Samson cleared his throat. "Argus saw three flotillas coming our way. Even with what defenses we can bring to bear, that may not be enough."

"If we do not stand against them, then who will?" demanded another voice, the hot-headed young man who'd spoken first. "I say we fight! Show those royal dogs the King's hand doesn't reach this far."

A mighty cheer followed his words, and from his corner Samson sighed. He knew advising caution was not to be borne, not when so many of the folk in this room had watched the Royal Navy take everything from them. Still, there was no sense in rushing towards ruination when it was coming right at you.

The men began talking, making plans for their glorious defense. Samson stood, limbs complaining at the movement, and turned to go when he heard Captain Crain call him over. The other man still stood near the front of the room, so Samson had to push his way through the crowd to reach him.

"Samson," Crain said, voice low. "Can I leave it in your hands to spread word for an evacuation? The women and children should be moved to the interior of the island. In case the battle goes ill."

The carpenter heard the unspoken words in the captain's sentence—not 'in case' but 'when'. Still, he nodded.

"Leave it to me."

Crain paused. "Will you tell *her* as well?"

"She is part of the community, too, Captain," Samson replied, knowing exactly whom Crain meant. Nadia was the oldest resident of Seaborne. She was also the most reclusive, rarely leaving her cottage up on the cliff.

"She won't go," Crain said seriously.

"I know." Samson sighed. "But I'll tell her, even so."

Samson moved more slowly than he would have liked through the town. His leg, aching from an old wound, complained with every step as he knocked on doors to spread word of the impending battle. Behind him came a stream of evacuees, fleeing for the desert hills further from the coast. Carts rolled over bumpy, dusty roads, and donkeys brayed as they were led towards the island's interior.

At last, having spread his message to enough folk that the whole town would soon hear of it, he paused to rest a while. Raising his eyes, Samson stared up the winding trail that led to the top of one of Seaborne's cliffs. A lonely cottage stood there, bent and gnarled as a weathered tree. He sighed. It was time to see Nadia.

The twisting path up to the clifftop was hundreds of steps, and Samson's leg ached with every one. He remembered the day he'd met Nadia. Everyone in town knew about her, of course. They called her a witch and a recluse, and Samson was fairly sure no one would care if she were to keel over in the town square. And yet, that day decades ago, she hadn't seemed a witch at all. Just a lonely woman. She'd stumped down to his carpenter's shop to get an old spindle repaired. A fine blue shawl had been thrown around her shoulders, and he hadn't been able to stop himself from asking where she'd gotten it. Such luxuries were comparatively rare in Seaborne.

Her eyes had shuttered. "I made it," she'd said, but there had been no pride or joy in her voice. Still, when Miriam Tassleton had been asking around for a new bedspread, it was Samson who'd made the trek up the cliff to ask Nadia if she might take the commission.

He made that same journey now, hoping the old spinster would speak with him. She was a wonder with all things fiber. She could patch a sail so the wind would never tear it again, and the ropes she knotted never frayed. Still, for all her talent, she kept everyone in town at arm's length, as though she disdained them all. He'd tried, on more than one occasion, to coax her down to Seaborne for a drink or during an open-air festival. But he'd never succeeded.

Samson crested the cliff with a heavy step. He took a few moments to gather himself before he crossed to the cottage, knocking hard on the crooked door.

"What?" Nadia's voice was like a cracking branch in a high wind. "What is it?"

"Nadia, it's Samson. Can I come in?"

A silence followed his question, and Samson bit back a sigh. Finally, a harried, "Oh, all right, then," came from behind the door, and the carpenter muscled it open.

Inside, the front room of the cottage looked like a flock of sheep had exploded. Baskets of fleece overflowed onto the floor, and lengths of yarn lay in tangled heaps in a trunk against the far wall. The room was stuffy, though the shutters of one of the windows were thrown open to overlook the sea, shedding light on a single skein of green yarn sitting on the windowsill. Beside it, Nadia sat on an overturned crate in front of her spinning wheel, that same, deep blue shawl she'd worn when he first saw her wrapped around her shoulders. Her face was craggy as the cliffside, and she frowned at him as he entered, each of her wrinkles deepening to a crevasse.

Samson grunted as he finally got through the door. He peered around the doorframe to where the top hinge hung loose.

"When did this happen?" he asked, fingers tracing the worn metal hinge. No wonder it had been so hard to open.

"What do you want?" Nadia demanded. "I haven't finished Alder's sail yet, if that's why you're here."

Samson considered the door. With the proper tools, he could probably fix it. He reached into his pocket, questing for screws—

"Leave it, carpenter."

"Nadia, you can't just leave your door broken."

"It's *my* door," she said crossly. "I'll do what I like with it."

"Fine," Samson said, stifling a sigh, "As you wish."

"What do you want?" she asked again.

"To warn you. The Royal Navy is coming to Seaborne. They may know the way through Rachim's Reef."

Samson did not know what he'd been expecting when he told her. It certainly wasn't the look of devastation that flitted across her face, hidden so quickly he briefly thought he'd imagined it. It was a look he knew well—many of Seaborne's residents arrived wearing it.

She turned away from him, her gaze tracking out over the sea. "Well," she said finally, "I suppose it's not unexpected."

Samson steeled himself. "Captain Crain has ordered an evacuation of the town. Some of the sailors are staying to fight."

That made Nadia turn. "They plan on fighting? With what? Sabers won't do much good against long guns, carpenter."

No, they wouldn't, but Samson didn't say that. Instead, he asked, "Will you leave? Head inland with the others?"

She frowned. "Will you?"

"What do you—"

"It is a fool's endeavor. You know that as well as I, better even. If the Royal Navy makes it through the reef, there will be no saving Seaborne, no matter how much fire the young folk down there have boiling in their blood."

He shook his head. "Seaborne means a great deal to them. It has been a refuge for many, including you. That means something."

Her frown darkened. "So you're not leaving."

"No. I'll not abandon them."

"Foolish," she muttered, turning away. "Go on, then."

"Will you—"

"I have no need to leave," Nadia interrupted. "They've already taken everything else from me. If the Navy seeks to burn me in my bed, I say let them try."

Samson winced. "There's no shame in running—"

"I will not run again," Nadia snapped. "Now leave."

Sighing, Samson turned back to the broken door, heaving it shut behind him.

It was midnight, Nadia was sixteen, and the ship was on fire.

She and her brother, Thomas, had booked passage on the *Abigail*. They'd been at sea eight days, passing beyond sight of land and out into the endless blue. Nadia had never been to sea before, and while she found it beautiful, she couldn't wait to reach their new home, a continent away.

But now, she and Thomas emerged from the belly of the ship to screaming and flames. Around them, a fearsome battle raged. Three ships of the line surrounded the small frigate, cannons ready to reduce the vessel to splinters. In the flash of gunfire, Nadia made out the brilliant red flag of the Royal Navy snapping in the wind.

There were many questions about that night to which Nadia never received answers. She never learned why the Navy targeted their ship. She never got the chance to ask Thomas how he knew exactly where the lifeboats were, or how far they were from their new home. But most of all, Nadia never knew if she would have acted differently, had she known what was to come.

Thomas got her settled in a lifeboat, swinging it out for the drop. Behind him, sailors were scattered across the deck, groaning and bloody.

His eyes had met hers from where he stood on the deck. "If I'm not back in five minutes, make the drop," he commanded.

"Thomas—" she started. She was only sixteen, and she was terrified.

"I'm going to try and save some of the others." He had to shout to be heard above the battle.

A colossal boom shook the ship, sending it tilting dangerously. Nadia reached out a hand, voicelessly pleading with her brother to leave them, to run. But he met her eyes, shaking his head.

"I have to try, Nadia. It's the right thing to do."

"No. No, Thomas!" Nadia screamed as her brother plunged back into the fray. She sat frozen in the boat, heart trying to pound itself out of her chest. She wanted to get up, to run after her brother and *make* him get in the boat, but she couldn't seem to move.

A sound like thunder tore through the air, and the deck buckled and split. The falls holding the lifeboat snapped, and Nadia screamed as she plummeted down towards the black sea. Her boat struck the side of the ship as it fell, and Nadia heard a sharp crack, like the sound of an axe striking wood. She had just enough time to see a fracture splinter down the middle of her lifeboat before the vessel hit the water with speed.

Nadia was drenched with salty spray. The ocean began leaking into the boat almost immediately. Behind her, the three Royal Navy vessels drew tighter around the burning *Abigail*.

"Thomas!" Nadia shrieked, her voice lost beneath the maelstrom of battle. "Thomas!"

The lifeboat was sinking, water sluicing in through cracks in the hull. Nadia fought to stay afloat, but water poured in faster than she could fling it out. The sea tossed her little vessel to and fro until it disappeared beneath the water. And Nadia, in her heavy wool skirts, was pulled down with it.

The world beneath the waves was cold and dark. Nadia fought against the water, trying desperately to claw back to the surface, to find something to hold onto, but nothing met her hands. Her lungs burned. Her vision began winking with black spots.

Fear, pain, and fury welled up inside her. Nadia opened her mouth, screaming into the sea. Water poured in between her teeth, down her throat, but she didn't care. If she were to die here, she would not go quietly.

The scream echoed in the deep, growing louder, as though something were screaming back. The blue-black world around her seemed to convulse. Through her darkening vision, she watched the water coalesce into the figure of a woman who hung suspended in the ocean a mere foot from where Nadia was drowning. She had hair as green as seaweed, and a gown of seafoam. She looked nearly human, until Nadia glanced into her eyes.

They were black as the depths of the sea, black as the sky at night. And they watched Nadia with unfathomable sadness.

The creature—the woman—reached out a hand and touched Nadia's breastbone. Beneath that touch, she felt her lungs expand with air, the water disappearing. She almost recoiled from the woman, recalling the tales of selkies and fair folk the servants used to whisper in the kitchen at night. Those black eyes bore into her, chilling her with their uncanny intelligence.

You wish to be saved.

The words reverberated in the ocean around her, more felt than heard. Nadia shuddered as those words crawled over her skin, but still she nodded.

What will you give me in payment for your life?

"Anything," Nadia said, the word leaving her mouth as bubbles. "Everything."

The woman regarded her with those deep, sad eyes, before nodding. Her seaweed-hair eddied around her with the motion.

Then Everything is what I will take.

The woman reached out once more, grasping Nadia's hands, and Nadia felt a sharp pain as though each palm had been cut. She pulled away, but there was nothing now to pull away from. The woman was gone.

Her lungs began burning once more as the water redoubled its efforts to swallow her. Frantically, Nadia twisted her hands upwards in the sea.

And the sea twisted back.

A rope of water, blue and cold, met her fingers. She grasped it and pulled herself upward, hand over hand, twisting more water into a rope, barely conscious of how she managed it. Her head broke the surface and she gasped, hacking up brine and salt. Her water rope was wrapped over a piece of planking, and she heaved herself onto it, sputtering and sobbing. She thrust the wet hair from her eyes, staring towards where the *Abigail* had been. A few smoldering boards floated on the water's surface, but the ship was entirely gone. In the distance, the Royal Navy vessels sailed away into the dark.

A storm was blowing in over the island. Its massive thunderheads were black against the blue sky. From her window, Nadia watched them roll in with a frown burrowing itself between her brows. Her fingers traced the twist of the green skein on the sill. The house seemed quiet and close, almost watchful.

I have to try, Nadia. It's the right thing to do.

She shook her head, seeking to dislodge the memories creeping into her mind. Perhaps the rain would dissuade those fools down in Seaborne, make them turn tail and run as they should. Or perhaps it would simply make their job that much harder.

I have to try, Nadia.

Thunder rolled overhead, sending a shudder through the cliff face and drawing Nadia's gaze back to the clouds. They swung low, heavy with water they'd start dumping soon enough.

I have to try.

"Are you ever quiet?" she snapped into the empty air. No one responded, of course. She shut her eyes, breathing out through her nose.

Nadia often thought about that night, about what she had done and what she had not. The woman in the water, her green hair eddying around her like seaweed, had indeed taken everything: Thomas, and with him the new home they'd been sailing towards, had been eaten by the waves. But the power given to her to save her life had never departed, though Nadia had never known what to do with it. She'd always been a gifted spinner, but since that night her spinning went beyond silk and cotton. After Thomas had died, she'd spun her grief into a soft, silky yarn from which she'd knit a deep blue shawl. From her fury, she'd spun a wild red yarn and woven the blankets on her bed. And from the shameful relief at her escape, she'd spun the seaweed-green yarn that rested upon her windowsill, where she could see it every day.

It had been Samson who first noticed her spinning, and Samson who began bringing her the work of the town. At first, she'd thought to turn him away, but she had needed the money more than she'd needed her pride. She'd taken the work of torn sails and ripped shawls from the carpenter, whose kind eyes and patience reminded her, painfully, of Thomas. With such work to do, she had stopped spinning impossible things, trading them for wool and flax, silk and cotton.

She'd stopped, but she hadn't forgotten.

"Damn it," she muttered, turning away from the window. Her wheel sat behind her, accusing her with its stillness, and she sighed. Then she went to heave open her door.

Wind whipped through Nadia's hair as she slowly pulled her spinning wheel out into the storm. After she'd set it on the cliff's edge, she went back for the crate. Her back throbbed with the strain, yet still she dragged the thing behind her, warped wood digging into the dirt of the cliff until it came to rest before the wheel. She settled herself atop it and looked up to the roiling gray clouds above. She'd failed Thomas once. She wouldn't fail again.

Nadia remembered when her grandmother had taught her how to spin. The old woman's fingers had shown her how to pinch the fleece, how to draft it for a fine thread or a thick one, how to send the spindle turning. She remembered her childhood hands, chubby and clumsy, spinning wool with a spindle that wouldn't stop wobbling.

"Be patient," her grandmother had chided when Nadia pouted at her work, so ugly compared to her grandmother's supple yarn. "These things take time."

"These things take time," Nadia muttered to herself as she reached up into the sky. With deft hands, she pinched out a piece of low-hanging cloud, pulling it down. She drafted it out, wrapping it around the leading string of her old wheel. A quick press of her foot on the treadle, a twitch of her hand on the flywheel, and the spinning wheel jumped into motion, twisting the gathered clouds into a fine, silky yarn the color of the sea after a storm.

Nadia pulled the clouds from the sky with skillful, creaking hands. Her back ached, and her fingers grew numb with the cold, yet still she spun, pulling down handfuls of the storm and winding them onto the bobbin. When each bobbin grew full, she stopped, detaching it from the wheel to tuck away in a sack at her side and replace it with another before she began again.

She was on the last bobbin, clouds gliding smoothly through her hands, when she heard the crack. She grasped the wheel, stopping its motion, and stared down towards the maidens that held her bobbin in place. A fracture ran down the left one, slithering all the way to the base. Her fingers tightened on the wheel. She hadn't considered what the water from the clouds might do to the wood.

Releasing the last bit of cloud back to the sky, Nadia ran a finger over the crack, feeling absurd tears building behind her eyes. It was just a spinning wheel, she told herself. It was just the wheel she'd spun on since Thomas's death. It shouldn't matter. Still, there was a painful knot welling in her throat as she realized the wheel was, more than likely, beyond repair.

Carefully, she detached the last bobbin from its place, stowing it in her pocket. With a final look at the crack in her wheel, she stood. Fetching her cane from the cottage and hefting her sack with the other bobbins, she turned and began the long trek down to the seawall.

Samson was tired. His leg smarted and his fingers hurt from an afternoon and evening spent preparing for the assault. Most of the men were asleep, looking like gray wave caps beneath their blankets as they lay along the top of the wall. Samson picked his way among them, trying not to trip. He glanced up at the black sky. He'd expected rain, had seen the storm clouds gathering all afternoon, but they'd dissipated during the evening and into the night, never dropping even a thimbleful of liquid. The stars glinted above, bright eyes ready to watch Seaborne fight and fall.

Captain Crain stood alone near one of the seawall's stairs, his gaze hard on the ocean. Samson came to stand beside him.

"How's the night?" Samson asked softly.

"Still," the captain replied. "Too still for my liking."

"Have they been spotted?"

The captain shook his head, beaded braids clattering together. "No. But dawn is still some ways off. We will stand ready until then."

Samson nodded, turning to gaze to the water. All was dark and quiet, and nervous fear curdled in his gut at the quiet. The fleet would be here, sooner or later. Then they would find out if the firepower of Seaborne would be enough.

"Move, or I'll move you."

Starting, Samson turned towards the seawall's stairs. There, at the base of the staircase with a bag slung over her shoulder, was Nadia. She was glaring at the guard posted there, her gaze enough to turn a lesser man to stone.

"Grandmother, I told you, this is—"

Her eyes flicked up and caught Samson's gaze. "Carpenter!" she yelled. "Tell this man to stand aside, or he'll learn exactly what a cane to the head feels like."

Samson was already hurrying down the stairs. "It's all right, I'll take care of it," he murmured to the stunned guard, who looked a little queasy from Nadia's dagger-like stare. He turned towards the spinster.

"What are you doing here?"

She huffed. "Why does everyone keep asking me that?"

Because it looks like a stiff wind could blow you over. "This is no place for an old woman," he tried.

She shook her head and shouldered past him. "It's no place for an old man either, carpenter. Give me your arm."

Samson wavered. He should force her to leave, to flee for safety inland. But it looked as though Nadia was getting up the stairs with or without his help, and he didn't want to be on the receiving end of any more of her ire. He hurried after her, offering his elbow and helping her to the top of the seawall.

The captain looked askance as they appeared, eyes darting first to Nadia and then Samson. "I thought she was to be evacuated."

"I tried," Samson muttered as Nadia released his arm and moved to the edge of the wall.

"What defenses do you have?" Nadia asked, her creaking voice taking on the sharp crack of authority.

Crain arched an eyebrow. "Twenty long guns. Thirteen cannon, though only enough shot for perhaps four rounds each. Muskets for the men."

"Hmph. That won't be enough."

The captain opened his mouth to reply when a shrill whistle cut through the air. All along the wall, men began sitting up, their gazes dragged towards the cliffs. Samson and Crain stiffened, and Nadia frowned.

"What was that?"

"The lookout," Crain said, mouth drawn in tight. "The fleet has been spotted."

"Then we haven't much time," Nadia said. She set her bag down and opened it, pulling out what looked like a bobbin wrapped thickly in silvery spider's web. "We can't let them reach the bay."

"We'll try to hold them off—"

"You needn't try," Nadia interrupted. "Just leave it to me." She plucked at the bobbin in her hands, pulling free a thread. Moving slowly, then growing faster, she began unspooling the thread, pushing it off the seawall. As she did, the cord unfurled, billowing out to become a dense cloud that skated down to the bay, hovering just above the water.

"It's fog," Samson breathed, eyes wide. It was impossible. And yet, she must have done it. No wonder the clouds above had thinned as the night wore on: Nadia had stolen them from the sky. He didn't know how she'd accomplished it, but she'd brought them exactly what they needed. A fog so dense that no ship—no fleet—could pass through it safely. Not with Rachim's Reef lurking in wait.

"Carpenter," Nadia snapped, continuing her unspooling. "Don't just stand there gawking. Hand me the next bobbin."

Samson jumped to obey, pulling out the next bobbin and handing it to her. Soon a fog thicker than wool was spreading down from the seawall, enshrouding the bay and the deadly reef beneath the water.

A few minutes later, two more sharp whistles pierced the air. Beside them, Captain Crain swore.

"They're at the reef's entrance," he muttered. "The fog hasn't reach that far yet."

"Bring me some of your men, Captain," Nadia commanded. "Let's see if they can unspool a bobbin as well as they can shoot a musket."

The captain nodded sharply. He began shouting orders, and soon Samson and Nadia had another six hands to them, unspooling the clouds down onto the water. The rest of the soldiers took up positions along the wall, and the rattle of cannons being moved and loaded cut through the otherwise silent night. The fog billowed from Nadia's hands, and before too long Samson could barely make out his own feet, let alone anyone further down the seawall.

A boom pierced the air. Around them, the soldiers tensed. Moments later came the distant splash of something heavy hitting water. Cannon shot.

"That's the last of it," Nadia said, holding up the final bobbin.

Samson nodded. "I can help you back down the steps."

"What? No. I'm not going, carpenter." The spinster turned her eyes towards the wall of fog before them. "I will see this through."

Samson wanted to argue, even opened his mouth to do so, but something stopped him. Nadia seemed made of steel, and he feared how sharp she might be if he tried to move her. So he merely nodded.

Another boom came, then another. A murmur passed along the wall, soldiers shifting nervously. The fog was too thick for them to see anything, and sounds came through it muffled, so that where the shots came from or how distant they were was hard to tell. The night began to lighten as dawn approached, and still they waited. When at last the sun rose and began to burn away Nadia's fog, Samson could hardly believe his eyes.

There was a single ship in the bay. A single ship *only*. Behind it, distant among the shoals, he caught sight of masts sticking from the water like felled trees, torn sails hanging limply. The ragged remains of the force sent to destroy Seaborne, sliced to ribbons by Rachim's Reef and Nadia's fog.

"Prepare the long guns!" Captain Crain's shout echoed along the seawall, and a great cry rose from the sailors. Nadia watched without a word, her eyes bright. Tentatively, Samson reached for her hand. To his surprise, she reached back and gripped him tightly. He glanced down at her and realized why her eyes looked so bright—tears shone in them, unspent.

"I thought it would feel better," she murmured. "Having my revenge."

Sailors and soldiers eddied around them, but Nadia and Samson stood alone, rocks among the tide. The carpenter studied her, his gaze thoughtful.

"How *does* it feel?" he asked.

"Like I've taken the knife used against me and turned it on another." She swallowed. "Even if in defense, I can't say I like the feeling."

"I can take you back up the cliffs, Nadia."

"No," she said, shaking her head. "I will stay to see what I've wrought."

She would not move, and so Samson did not either. Even as the booms of the first long guns shook the stones beneath their feet, the spinster and the carpenter stood side by side, watching as the last ship was burned in the bay.

Nadia sat in her cottage, running her old hands over the crack in the spinning wheel. Only a day had passed since she had unleashed her fog. A day since she had repaid Thomas's death a hundredfold. After the battle in the bay—if a battle it could be called—she had gone back up the cliff alone. Samson might have gone with her, if she'd asked, but she hadn't wanted him to. She could not say she regretted what she'd done, but so many lives lost to her strange magic weighed heavy on her hands.

She gently touched the crack on her wheel once more before she sighed, turning to the window. The skein of green yarn seemed to wink at her from where it lay on the windowsill, and she picked it up. It would be a good while until she could spin again. She'd have to see about a new wheel. Perhaps she could knit something to pass the time.

There was a knock on her door, and she frowned. "What? What is it?"

A grunting sounded, the door being shoved open, and Samson appeared. He gave her a tired smile. "I expected you to be sleeping off your heroic efforts," he said. "Instead, I find you before your wheel. As ever."

"What do you want, carpenter?" Nadia demanded. "Is there yet another platoon or something on the way?"

He chuckled. "No, certainly not. I wanted to check on you. Make sure you're all right."

"Of course I am."

"Of course," he parroted. His thoughtful eyes examined her, and Nadia fought the urge to squirm beneath their appraisal. "You know," he said after a moment, "we would not have won the battle without you."

"No, you would not have."

He cocked his head. "How did you do it?"

"Do what?"

He sighed. "Nadia, please."

Nadia pursed her lips. "How do you make a table? Or an oar?"

"Time," he said. "Time and practice."

"Then you know how I spun the storm," she replied. It was only partly a lie.

She examined Samson more closely, seeing a heavy-looking bag in his hands. "What's that you've got?"

He hefted it up. "Supplies. For your door."

"I told you to leave it."

"You did," he agreed slowly. "But I've decided not to listen. You need a working door, Nadia. Sometime soon, you may actually want to let someone in."

She opened her mouth to object. After all, perhaps she *liked* to have a door that kept solicitous neighbors at bay. But she found the words would not come.

"Fine, carpenter," she said eventually. "As you wish. You can fix the door. Just don't make too much noise."

"I wouldn't dream of it," Samson said, smiling, before he turned back to the broken hinge.

From where she sat beside the window, Nadia watched him thoughtfully. He had a good complexion for green, she thought, especially the paler shade she now held in her hands. Besides, it was a long, cold trek up the cliff. He could certainly use a scarf.

See J.C. Pillard's story "The Spinster and the Sea" online at Metaphorosis.
If you liked it, leave a comment. Authors love that!
Remember to subscribe to our e-mail updates so you'll know when new stories are posted.

About the story

This story can be partially blamed on Tamora Pierce and her *Circle of Magic* series. If you haven't read Tamora Pierce, then please put this down and go pick up one of her tales right now! The *Circle of Magic* series was some of the first YA I ever read, and the first book of the series, *Sandry's Book*, focuses on the titular character and her ability to use spinning to work magic. Pierce herself has spoken about viewing handcrafts as a kind of magic, and I remember reading that book and being downright envious of Sandry's ability to create with her hands.

I did, eventually, learn some handcrafts myself. I started knitting years ago and spinning this past year. One of my friends possesses a spinning wheel, and very kindly let me try it. (She also took a look at an earlier draft of the story to make sure my terminology was right—thank you, Laura!) While using that wheel, I was reminded of *Sandry's Book*, and the question of what magical spinning would look like popped into my mind once more, planting the first seeds of this tale. Magical spinning, I reasoned, would spin impossible things, like sadness and rage and storms. And what better place to spin a storm than on a cliff, overlooking the sea?

Nadia, my main character, came to me almost fully formed—angry and isolated and nursing an old wound. I loved the idea of a woman whose spinning is both the source of her power and the source of her isolation. For that reason, Nadia is not the first character we meet. She is alone within the tale, both literally and figuratively, and it takes another craftsperson to make her face that fact. The story can only resolve once Nadia acknowledges that she's the source of her own problem. It is only through that acknowledgement that Nadia is able to use her power for something greater than herself.

A question for the author

Q: Aliens, are they out there?

A: Probably. The visible universe has over 400 quadrillion stars in it, and if even a tiny fraction of those stars have a planet that could support life…well, a tiny fraction of a gigantic number is still a gigantic number. I think it would be rather anthropocentric to imagine we're the only life, or even the only intelligent life, in the cosmos.

So yeah, they're probably out there. Maybe they'll even read this story one day. If so, hi! What took you so long?

About the author

J.C. Pillard is an author and editor living at the foot of the Colorado Rockies. She's an avid reader and writer of speculative fiction, and particularly loves anything folklore-inspired. When she's not writing, J.C. spends her time knitting and playing D&D. She's also recently taken up spinning, which might explain this story.

www.jcpillard.com, @JCPillard

Sturm und Clang

Sara Kate Ellis

"Just use your homespun innocence, Sam. Those townies will trust you."

"Homespun, Barry? Really?" Sam says. "It's more like Pottersville from *It's a Wonderful Life.* Only without the fun."

Barry's her editor at *Pitch Magazine*, the West Coast's foremost—which means surviving—music magazine, but for an editor, he's surprisingly averse to details. She stares out the Lyft window at the dry, sunlit malaise of Felder's Pike, sees a nail salon and a boarded-up tax office, probably once a thriving brick-and-mortar. On the corner, a payday loan shop hides the thinly painted-over logo of a Starbucks that must have ducked in and out of the town within a season, and Hoagie's Diner, where her favorite band *The Waffle Irons* used to hang out after shows. Now it's a tavern with tinted windows and an entrance scattered with cigarette butts.

"Well, then, push the dying Americana angle," Barry says. "Get a feel for what was there. The sweetness. A look back at an America when it was okay to be aspirational."

He says it like it never was okay to be aspirational, but now that the danger's passed, he's willing to indulge the idea a little. Sam reaches into her handbag, brushing her fingers against her Tic Tac container of edibles for reassurance. Barry's never liked *The Waffle Irons*, just like most people don't like *The Waffle Irons*, but with the death of Mapes Higgins, the band's last living member, his hand has been forced. And Sam, much to her surprise, has just touched down to write a three-thousand-word feature, her biggest for the magazine yet.

She glances at the file she's brought with her, printed out so she doesn't have to squint at her phone. A photocopy of the old liner notes to a reissue of their album sneers up from the page.

'Wherefore art My Roameo' evinces the loneliness and confusion experienced by those average girls, unwillingly thrust into the music business and their strange brand of stardom. They were an amalgam of the everygirl. Not too pretty, but not homely either. Plump in that charming way of girls in farming communities, with the unambitious dreams of homemaking and boys.

Ugh.

"A nice memorial," Barry says. "We'll throw in some copy about Niles Deep."

There it is. The real reason Sam's here. Niles Deep, an algorithm in the guise of a soulfully bland white boy, just namedropped the song in his latest hit, 'Cool Run Deep'.

Wherefore art my Roameo
I'm here yo! I'm here yo!

Sam's not thrilled her chance to write about her favorite band has been generated by a bot-thario, but she'll take it. She's twenty-eight, still paying off loans in a rent-controlled apartment, and her mother is telling her to take up teaching. Poor man's Pottersville or not, she's come to find redemption or a recharge. Or something.

"A nice hometown memorial," Barry says. "Have it to me by Monday."

The first time Sam heard the *Irons*, she laughed like everyone else, played the LP once more out of disbelief, and then—telling herself it was for kicks—listened repeatedly until each song became an earworm. Either the girls—Mapes, Amy, and Edith — were geniuses, or they were the worst band in the world. Most critics bent toward the latter, describing their sound as "a nasal cacophony whose key changed like the Dow during a meltdown... a nonsensical mishmash of teenage melodrama mixed with plain Jane reserve." They were the garage band that never quite made it out of the garage, so bad they were brilliant. This was why Gen X women loved them. This is why Sam, a Millennial or a Zennial—that window keeps changing—loves them, too.

Her first stop is Felder's Pike High, the girls' erstwhile, not-quite alma mater. Ingrid Bevan, former Mapes classmate now school counselor, is giving her the grand tour.

"Not a lot of folks around here care for their music much, to be honest," she says. She leads her to a display case in the double-load corridor, her expression somewhat apologetic. "But we're proud of them all the same."

A few ribbons and photographs are pinned haphazardly to a felt board. There's an old black and white of *The Waffle Irons* jammed in between one of a winning golf team and someone taking a second-place award in a national speech contest.

"What was it like?" Sam asks. "On their last day?"

The story goes that their father Ward, a government contractor, cracked after tanking his portfolio. His solution? A get-rich-quick scheme involving a truckload of cheap instruments and pulling Mapes, Edith, and Amy out of school. From then until his death in the Bechlan asylum three years later, the girls spent their days isolated, practicing instruments and holding concerts at birthday parties and the Runyon Community Center. Preparing for a big break that never happened. The girls released one album with a print run of two thousand copies. It got little to no airplay and they never released a second, although they were working on it. Sam's got a few pages of the sheet music copied from the U.C.L.A. archive, scrawled by hand in a million different colors, and despite Barry's trivialization of the assignment, she harbors a secret hope she may unearth the rest.

Bevan shrugs. "They were pretty circumspect, but that was how those girls were. Honestly, I think Mapes was happy about it. She didn't get along with the teachers here."

"Really?" Sam's eyes drift over the photo: the girls hunched up on the stage, their instruments surrounding them like oversized luggage. They don't look much like rebels. Ward even boasted something to that effect in the liner notes, how they were 'counter to the counter culture'.

"Mapes was too smart." Bevan says. She glares at a pair of boys as they scurry past her down the corridor, late for class. "All three of them were. Mapes and Edith were already taking classes at the local college."

"College?" Sam turns back to her, blinking in surprise. "And Ward allowed it?"

Bevan waves her off like it's obvious. "Of course. He talked the college into letting them attend."

Sam takes this in as Bevan directs her to a set of carpeted stairs at the end of the hall.

"Do you know what they were studying?"

She expects to hear something like Intro to Accounting or Home Management, but Bevan smiles a little wryly, as if Sam's response was predictable.

"Advanced calculus, linear algebra, that kind of stuff. Mapes used to really tick off our math teacher, Mr. Dredley. She was way ahead of him." She stops before a set of heavy doors. "Here we are."

Sam shakes off her confusion. Nearly everything she's read about the band alludes to their averageness. Their being torn from school itself was never treated as a squelching of their potential, but the deprivation of what middling observers might refer to as a 'normal life'. She reminds herself to ask Bevin more questions later, but right now she's got to focus. The shop class is part of *Irons* lore. It's where the girls played their last show, unbeknownst to their father, returning on the day that, had they stayed enrolled, would have been Amy's last as a senior. Sam's got a lone, grainy black-and-white from the event. In it, the girls stand next to a boxy metal sculpture adorned with vacuum tubes and wires. Their instruments and amplifiers flank the trio like lumpish rooks.

"I wasn't there," Bevan sighs. "But the girls came in during the final class period, locked the room, set up, and started playing. Principal Mosier chewed them out and kept their equipment impounded for a couple of weeks, but not much else. Didn't tell their Dad on them."

"Nice of him," Sam says.

Bevan shrugs, a mix of sour and sad puckering her features. "He knew what they were dealing with at home."

The concert was just a few days before Ward checked into the asylum. Did the sisters sense a weakness and act on it?

She takes in a breath, readying herself for her *Abbey Road* moment, but the room Bevan opens up on lies strictly in the present. Bright halogen spills over row upon row of kids with anime hairstyles, all clacking away at their laptops. A clash of midis and dub beats and vocoder outbursts pings around the room like cannon fire. It's music, or a semblance of it, but it scrapes against Sam's eardrums like a saw blade. She's been on her share of music pilgrimages, The Motown Museum, Hendrix's grave, and the old Satyricon club in Portland, but she doesn't think she's ever been more disappointed. It's as if Niles Deep and his algorithms have usurped this part of the *Irons*' story too.

"Kind of like stepping onto the Tardis, I imagine," Bevan says, a hint of pride in her voice. "It's a computer lab now."

Sam's about to press her hands to her ears, but she stops herself as she takes in the equally confused gaze of the instructor, a dark-haired, bespectacled woman who slaps her laptop shut as if they've caught her running a search on homemade explosives.

"What is this, Ingrid?" She's clearly not happy about the intrusion.

Bevan plants a palm across her forehead. "Oh, my word, I forgot to tell you. Florence, this is—"

Sam crosses between them, offering her hand. "Sam Taber from *Pitch* magazine."

The woman bends over her desk to take it, her grip hard and a mild scowl tugging at her lips. She's buttoned-up yet effortless, in a denim shirt and dockers, a cross between a schoolmarm and a Silicon Valley hopeful. Sam suspects she must have seven exact copies of that outfit in her closet.

"Flo Nagourney." Her eyes drop to Sam's Tee with its bright orange logo reading *Gabba Gabba Hey!*

"This is where *The Waffle Irons* used to hang out," Bevan says. She's already backing toward the door. "I thought I'd—"

"Them?" Flo says. She trains her gaze at some kids in the back of the classroom. "I hear Fortnite, Georgi!" She glares. "And Davis! Update your fic later. I want those loops coded before the bell." She rolls her shoulders back and turns to face Sam. "That's fine, but my kids are up to their ears in Sonic Pi, so it would be great if you could make this quick."

"Not a problem," Sam says.

In fact, she's more than happy to oblige.

Bevan coughs out a quick excuse, ducking out as the din starts up again. Flo doesn't move, however. She's still staring at Sam like an object that doesn't sit right on the mantel.

"Guess this isn't what you came for," she says.

"Not... really," Sam says, a little disconcerted by the sudden awkwardness between them.

"Well..." Flo gestures to a pair of large sockets in the corner. "It's still got the wiring from the old days. I'll give it that. You could power an ENIAC in here."

"A what?"

Flo smiles, as if she shouldn't have expected Sam to get it. "An old mainframe." She looks back, somewhat ruffled. "So the *Irons*, huh?"

"Yeah."

"And someone's paying you for this?"

Flo eyes Sam's shirt again, and Sam can practically hear the calculations in her head. T-shirt plus age plus cheap sneakers equals eking out a freelancer's income at thirty.

"Take all the time you need," Flo says. "Got to get back to the real work."

She turns and leaves Sam in the corner with her face on fire.

Real Work.

She's still fuming in the Lyft to her next stop. Those are the same words her mother used, still uses to freeze her insides, dragging her back from that stubborn insistence—very lonely, very stubborn—that she has as much right to pursue a passion as the more privileged kids do. But she does get where this Flo person is coming from. In fact, what stuns her most about Ward's plan is less its ludicrousness than its relative viability. That in the late 1960s-early 1970s, the idea of getting rich off music was only moderately bonkers as opposed to downright delusional.

Imagine having a parent push you to be a musician. An artist, of any kind.

Just imagine.

Dave Blankenship, a former neighbor, still lives next door to the Higgins' old Victorian. It stands fenced in on the lot, sagging and condemned, but he's agreed to let Sam view it from his adjacent backyard.

There's been little upkeep. New battens and sarking boards have been patched in to keep out rain. The gabled roofs and spiny turrets have been dulled to nubs by time and neglect. But she can almost hear the clash of guitars against basement acoustics—Amy's drumbeats and the atonal chorus of 'Wherefore Art My Roameo'. He's one of the most enduring mysteries of the sisters' non-stardom. Roameo suspects have ranged anywhere from innocent crushes to older paramours and even a stray cat. The girls denied every theory.

"We already had a cat," Edith said. "And did you think we had time for boys?"

Blankenship has the look of an astronaut gone-to-seed, blotchy skin once pink with health, a belly pushing out the bright orange frond on the front of a Hawaiian shirt. He points through an opening in the fence between their properties where the boards have split off. "Mapes held on to the old place," he says. "Now she's gone, some upstart's gonna flip it."

Sam guesses that the properties in this town aren't that flippable, but she keeps that to herself. Ward Higgins was admitted to the Bechlan Asylum in the summer of 1969, and died there a year later. Edith and Amy went to live with an aunt on the other side of the country, while Mapes hitchhiked to the East Coast. She reappeared Heathcliff-like in the mid-1980s, rich off some investment, and moved a few things into the house, but didn't stay. It makes sense and no sense at the same time, Sam thinks, like some sad secret Mapes couldn't quite let go of.

"I used to sneak cigarettes to Mapes," Blankenship says. "She'd stand on a footstool and smoke them by the window and blame me when Ward asked about the smell." He chuckles at the memory. Sam's eyes follow the uneven concrete around the yard, now cracked with age and dandelions.

"Were you close?"

"Good friends," Blankenship says.

"Must have been friction, with all the noise."

He shrugs. "Most of the neighbors weren't so wound up about the music. There were lots of kids trying to be *The Beatles* back then. It was the other stuff."

"Other stuff?"

He squints up at the sky, frowns as if he senses rain. "Lots of banging around in the basement."

"Drums?" Sam's almost checked out on this guy, but there's a note in his voice that transcends bloviating.

"Nah." He shakes his head, almost bitterly, like the kid who was never asked to play. "They were working on something."

She squints at him, then stoops to peer through the fence again. "New material?" She knows this is not what he means.

He pauses and then leans in a little. "If you ask me, nothing good or the Feds wouldn't have taken Ward away. Searched the house too."

Sam steps back, a clipped bark of laughter escaping her. "Really?"

Blankenship could have spouted this story to any of the other journos who've come to cover the *Irons*, journos, who from their previous coverage would no doubt have added some condescending marginalia to their lore. But he's kept this one, waited until Mapes' death.

"Never saw what it was," Blankenship says. "Ward wouldn't let any of their friends get past the front door, but I will say this," he pauses, his Coke bottle lenses glinting with a kooky certainty. "The funny farm doesn't usually show up in suits and sedans."

Blankenship's likely just an attention seeker or a sincere oddball, but she does another search for Ward Higgins. The Bechlan Asylum shut its doors in the early '80s and was demolished in '87. But there's a name in an old article in a now defunct local paper, Shepley Labs. It was the last company Ward contracted with before he threw everything into the girls' music career, notable for a series of domestic computing flops, including a cooking computer and an early home playmate called My Buddy. She pulls up a page on dead technology, double-taking on an ad featuring a boxy thing with lightbulb eyes and a grille for a mouth.

A companion more faithful than Rover.
He stays here, while you go there.

The ad copy is close enough to the Irons' lyrics to give her pause.

Not one sold, the website says, but she wonders if it wasn't one of Ward's designs, a preview of failures to come. Or maybe he brought home a prototype. She looks at her watch, regrets not having asked Blankenship more questions. But it's late now, and her mind is churning and there's another place she needs to visit.

Hoagie's is what she expected from the outside, dim and grimy and reeking of snuck cigarettes, but after the weirdness with Blankenship, she's more than pleased with the obscurity. She takes a seat at the far end of the counter and orders a beer. Niles Deep's 'Cool Run Deep' dribbles from a candied-up retro jukebox in the corner, the *Irons*' lyrics followed by his dumbshit rejoinder.

> *While you Roam*
> *I'm at home*
> *I stay here, You go there*
> *No car, no bike, no feet, no wind*
> *Wherefore art my Roameo*
> *I'm here-yo!*
> *I'm here-yo!*

Thief.

The bartender brings her a Pabst. It's flat, but she downs half of it, her shoulders loosening with the buzz. She's about to order a shot when she hears a throat clear and turns to see Flo watching her from a darkened booth nestled behind her.

What's next? she wonders. Her mother walking through the door with a circled ad for entry-level daycare?

They stare at each other for a cold minute. Then Sam lets out a breath and tries, if not a smile, then a conciliatory nod. "Didn't seem like the type for this kind of place." She gestures to the stack of neglected worksheets next to Flo's beer glass. "I mean, with all that real work and all."

Flo shoots her a 'you got me' look and shrugs. "Here's to ladies loitering in ice cream parlors." She lifts her glass and gestures for Sam to join her.

Sam regards her suspiciously for another second. This has a strong whiff of all those times she ran into the cool kids outside of high school and they were inexplicably nice until Monday rolled around. But she grabs her bag and her beer and the gratis basket of popcorn and sits down with Flo in the booth.

"Bad day?"

Flo snorts. "You get warned about a lot of things before you become a teacher, but not that people have mistaken acronyms for algorithms. They really think that kids memorizing their ESLERS and IPFs means they'll automatically know how to conjugate French verbs or enter a Python value." She takes another long pull of her beer. "Even algorithms need content to work with."

"Even that?" Sam nods up at the speakers. Niles Deep's voice is oozing out of them like soft cream.

Flo shrugs, takes another sip of her beer. "Especially that. The formula's been built on thousands of previous successes."

Her tone is more philosophical than argumentative, but Sam's had enough of numbers and success metrics. "Not everything needs a formula."

"The *Irons* could have used one."

Sam doesn't deign to answer that. She senses Flo's eyes on her, feels her deciding in that minute to dial things down.

Flo leans forward, her weight on her elbows. "Honest question, and I don't mean reply guy honest. How can you stand them? The noise? Those listless voices?"

When people ask, Sam usually goes on the defensive. She'll talk about their lack of hipster disaffection, argue that they've got a genuine it-is-what-it-is quality that outshines the grandiose white dude pronouncements of songs like 'Let it Be' or 'Do You Realize'—the latter being the most cloying demand to smile she's ever heard. But from the beginning, their music tugged at something else inside her, an assurance that it was okay to be bad. That it was okay to make the wrong moves, because if you kept going, you might just land on the right ones. And if you didn't? At least they were yours.

"They..." she wraps her fingers around her glass. "I guess they're proof it's not too late, that you can suck by other people's standards and still stumble onto something beautiful."

Flo gives a half-smile, thoughtful but unconvinced. "Sounds like flailing."

"Flailing, huh?" Sam reaches for her backpack, pulls out that file she's been carrying around with her like a complex. "How about I show you something?"

She rifles through the mess until she finds what she's looking for: the photocopies of Mapes' sheet music. They're hand-written and color-coded, with so many looping scrawls across the page, you can barely see where the music starts and stops. "One of the greatest misconceptions about the *Irons*..." She wipes the condensation from the table before resting the pages on its surface. "... is that they were clueless kids banging out random notes. But Mapes and Edith wrote all the music out first. They wrote and rewrote it until it was just the way they wanted it. They weren't flailing. But they weren't imitating or running on some soulless program either. That's the difference."

She nudges the pages in front of her, a chaos of slashes and looping notations, and watches as Flo goes quiet. Her expression is humoring at first, and then that smile disappears.

"You sure?" she says, not dismissively this time, but like she's working out a problem.

"About what?" Sam says.

Flo runs her finger down to a series of slashes and numbers at the bottom of the page. She's staring at it with a mix of bemusement and fascination. "This kind of looks like score."

"That's what I mean," Sam says. "They compos—"

"No, I mean SCORE," Flo says. "A musical notation program. The first." She pushes up her glasses, and lifts the page for a closer look. "It started in '67, but it sure as hell wasn't *this* far along then. When did they write this?"

Sam hesitates, not ready for this sudden show of interest. "Late '69 or '70. Why?"

Flo doesn't answer and Sam doesn't press her. She's experiencing that vertigo when you realize you've gotten someone wrong. Flo's looking at her with the same expression.

"Mind if I copy these?" Flo asks.

"Sure," Sam says. "What for?"

Flo takes a long slug from a tepid water glass she's been ignoring.

"I'm not sure yet," she says.

Sam wants to think she's impressed her, that some part of Florence Nagourney caught a glimpse of the *Irons'* genius. In her room, she runs a search for SCORE and finds Flo isn't far off at all. SCORE got its start at Stanford in '67, two years before Ward pulled the girls out of school. Sam doesn't get coding, but the notations from the early incarnations seem rudimentary compared to the ornate chaos of Mapes' sheet music. Was the music part of a program? Was Ward teaching them programming language in addition to the music? Sam paces in the cramped space between the bed and the radiator. Wishes she'd gone right past Blankenship into the house.

Her phone buzzes, loud. She picks it up, her heart stalling as she hears Barry on the other end. He rarely bothers her during a story unless it's bad news.

He gets right to the point, too. "We're going to have to cut your piece down." He sounds exhausted, like this is the last among hundreds of similar calls.

"How much?"

"A thousand words. I'll throw in an extra ten cents per word. I didn't want to do this, Sam. Niles Deep has an album about to drop with 'Cool Run Deep'. Nothing confirmed yet, but I've got to be ready for it."

She doesn't protest. No buts. There's no arguing with Barry. She just asks another question.

"Did you know the girls were smart?"

"Ha. Funny."

"I mean like brilliant smart. Ward wasn't homeschooling them. Not really. They were going to college and—"

He laughs again, as if this time, she's gotten him. "Who've you been talking to? Look, we're not looking for Jim Morrison here. Just a nice, sweet story about some girls with stars in their eyes, okay? I'll see you Monday."

The next question dies in her throat.

The Runyon Community Center is one of the only *Irons* performance venues still standing. She's got more than enough material to cover the meager word count Barry's affording her—she's much more worried about affording rent—but she'll be damned if she misses this, for if there's anything remaining of the *Irons'* dissonant spirit, it's here. The stage is rickety, the floorboards sunken and listing toward the exit. For a few minutes, she thumbs in her earbuds and revels in the lopsidedness of it all.

> *Who you are, where you come from*
> *Who really can care*
> *When you've got*
> *The family that's there?*

For a few minutes, the Caligari angles fulfill their promise. She's back amid the jeers and the sweat, the tossed soda cans and doomed-to-fail expectations of nearly every teenage rite of passage. Maybe it's the old school smell of wood and scuffed sneakers, or the growing darkness blurring the edges of past and present, but she catches that ineffability, the flicker not so much of promise, but of the possibility that comes from the decision just to try.

Sam still wants to try. She's close to finding something that's hers; it's the world that keeps giving up on her. This time when her phone rings, she doesn't answer.

She only notices Flo's message after she's played the album all the way through.

[Mind coming by the school? I'd like you to hear something].

It's a long weekend with no kids around, and when the security guard leads her to the lab, it feels portentous, not at all like the dry disappointment of the other day. She can already hear a clip of 'My Confidant' playing on a loop, Amy's stroppy drumbeats warring with Mapes' and Edith's oscillating chord progressions.

> *On the stairs,*
> *Under the chair,*
> *You're there*
> *Even in my hair*

Flo turns down the volume and gestures for her to come in. "Sorry for calling you out of the blue like that," she says. "I worried you'd leave town."

There's an agitation in her movements that wasn't there yesterday, like a movie where an old curmudgeon switches bodies with a hip teen. She puts a hand on the back of her chair, swivels it absently back and forth, like she's deliberating. "Their music. It's interesting."

Sam coughs out a laugh. "Is that so?"

"I didn't say 'good'," Flo says, pulling into herself again. "But..." She turns up the volume, lets the rest of 'My Confidant' blare, messy and discordant. "Beginners make predictable music. Same three chords. Same harmonies. But hear that? That quick rise over the dominant chord as it slides up again and then back down for no apparent reason?"

"Ah," Sam says. "So you've got scientific proof that they suck?"

Flo waves off her remark, winces at feedback screech. "No. I mean, maybe. Ever hear of a Markov chain?"

"Not really," Sam says.

"It's a process that lays out a sequence of possibilities, with the probabilities always based on the event before it. They use it for weather, traffic flow, and to replicate the style of a composer. I input the *Irons* music to a program I've been tweaking. You'd better sit down for this."

What comes next is a revelation. It's a version of their music: the chaos, those wildly fluctuating sequences are still there, but each variation mingles perfect harmony with perfect discord, a balance where none should be. Sam's always heard this in their music and struggled to explain it, but here that euphony jumps out, a clear pattern running through the drumbeats and the melody, steady and endless and unforeseeable.

"I expected something roughshod," Flo says, lowering the volume. "Simple and predictable, but with this... every deviation evokes a myriad of other departures." She draws back, face drawn; her dark eyes are brimming with excitement. "I didn't mean to make things sound so soulless the other night. I was feeling pretty soulless myself, to be honest, but this is something special, Sam."

Sam feels a flutter of something roll through her, a faint reverberation of the music.

"Do you..." she says. "Do you maybe want to break into a house?"

At night, the Higgins' Victorian looks a little more forbidding; the paint is faded and chipping, blending into the overcast sky as if a shift in the clouds might cause it to flicker from view. They creep through Blankenship's driveway, squeezing safely through the hole in the fence without incident. Sam starts for the front of the house, but Flo gestures toward the same basement window through which Blankenship passed his contraband soda and cigarettes. If they keep it quiet, they should be able to carry this off.

Flo fishes a flathead screwdriver from the pocket of her denim jacket. "I jump motherboards with these all the time," she whispers, slipping the tip under the window beading. Rot has set in the wood, leaving only a thin line like black mold on caulk that gives easily. She slips the screwdriver beneath the glass and nudges it from the weather-damaged frame.

"You want to go first?" she says.

Sam doesn't mind if she does.

The basement is a showroom of her expectations: a time capsule of wood paneling, low-ceilings, and yellow carpet muted into blood orange by the darkness. This is where it happened, where Ward exiled his daughters, and where they practiced their instruments until their fingers bled.

Flo tracks the flashlight along the walls, across the pencil marks marking their heights in a doorframe, that long series of befores. The paneling's been stripped from the back wall along with a large block of carpet, revealing an expanse of pocked concrete and exposed wiring.

"They were powering something bigger than a few guitars," Flo says, nodding at a series of cupholder-sized outlets, their mouths worn and blackened from use. In the corner, obscured by a tangle of hippy beads, is a large, blocky shadow.

Sam freezes, afraid this will be nothing, another grandiose overture that flops into a limping coda, but Flo's fingers find hers, tugging her forward as she casts her beam over a surface of dark chrome. It's a cabinet, the interior a hybrid from a mad scientist movie and some old timey player piano. Row upon row of bulbs and buttons peer from inside like some primordial, eye-studded creature. Vacuum tubes sag from its sides like limp appendages. She flashes back to that shop class photo, that strange, cumbersome thing near the amplifiers. There's a resemblance to the *My Buddy* model, but this is a bigger, far more complicated beast.

Bevan's and Blankenship's words come back to her.

Mosier kept their equipment impounded for a couple of weeks...didn't tell their Dad on them. Mapes was too smart.

They were building something.

"While you roam, I'm at home," she whispers. "They must have known those men were coming for Ward. They hid it at the school because they knew Mosier wouldn't contact him. And what self-respecting G-Man would suspect a trio of dopey girls capable of creating—" The words stop in her throat. She doesn't have them. Not yet.

Flo lets out a low whistle in accompaniment as she reaches over, her fingers trailing under a dusty cylinder of paper marked up in Mapes' chaotic hand.

No car, no bike, no feet, no wind.

"It was them," Sam says.

"Who?" Flo's gaze follows hers down to a faint scrawl at the bottom of the page.

> *Your Roameos,*
> *Mapes, Edith, and Amy.*

It's not a *My Buddy*, but a much larger version of it, more eyes, a larger grille for a mouth regarding them without judgment. Like it's been waiting for them all along.

On the drive back, they park the car at the edge of Goddard Lake.

The moon's out and the air has just enough chill to add a bite to their exuberance. They stay close to the car, not daring to risk the moldering treasure in the trunk; the books and papers, and the old and very heavy Disc Pack Flo jimmied out with her screwdriver. It's what they could carry away safely, but already Flo is talking about going back, even about putting down an offer on the house if she can scrape together the money. She's pacing back and forth as she talks.

"Hear of Alan Turing?" Flo turns to her, her voice shaky. They could both use a drink.

"Saw the movie."

"The good one with Derek Jacobi?"

"The lousy one with Benedict Cumberbatch."

She laughs, but something unspoken passes between them, an acknowledgement of what already feels steady, a routine. Flo is rigid and methodical, and much more in control of her life, but to Sam, she's a much-needed constraint in her algorithm.

"He built this monstrosity called the Aural Artefact," she says. "Programmed in the British National Anthem and Glenn Miller and..." She leans back against the hood of the car. "It was the first recording of computer-generated music, and it sounded awful, like a pipe blowing a raspberry." She slips her hands into her pockets. "But it reminded me of the *Irons*... There's a lassitude there, like the machine just wasn't in the mood." She takes in a breath, her dark eyes now deep with possibility.

"Look," Flo says. "I am not even close to understanding this, only that there's a lot more to this than a trio of girls and a failed music career, and..." She raises her hand, her smile flat as if she's growing impatient with herself. "I don't mean it that way. It's just that if you want someone to help you uncover the rest... I mean, I—I'd like to. Very much."

Sam feels the warmth travel to her cheeks. "Like maybe uncovering the shocking revelation that Roameo wasn't a boy?"

"Or a cat," Flo says.

"You've done your homework."

"I'm a teacher," Flo says. "I lead by example."

They grin at each other, bodies loosening as they meet in the middle. Sam doesn't worry about her mother or the thousand words she's got to plunk out by Monday. Barry will get what he wants: a phoned-in cutesy retrospective on three hapless, dopey girl musicians. And sure, Sam might even have to work in retail for a spell, but failure's just another disguise when they don't know what's coming.

She's got a real story now, about three girls in isolation; three lonely geniuses who built a friend and a collaborator, creating music into which the four of them could pour their loneliness. Art out of circumstances. It's a much better story than the one even the *Irons'* well-intentioned champions assigned to them;

much better than the one she's assigned to herself.

And on the drive back, when Niles Deep's 'Cool Run Deep' drips from the radio, she finds herself singing along.

See Sara Kate Ellis's story "Sturm und Clang" online at Metaphorosis.
If you liked it, leave a comment. Authors love that!
Remember to subscribe to our e-mail updates so you'll know when new stories are posted.

About the story

This story came from an obsession with the rock trio, *The Shaggs*. Like Sam, I cackled the first time I heard one of their songs, but by the third play, the smugness had left the building. There's a genuine mystery behind their appeal: Is it the jagged unpredictability in their melodies? Or the way the drummer sounds like she's accompanying a different album altogether? But it wasn't until a few years after being introduced to them that I caught something A.I.-like in their atonality. So, the basis for the story began with a question: What if the 'Foot Foot' in "My Pal Foot Foot" (Roameo in the story) were really a sentient machine's term for human beings? And what if that machine were grappling with loneliness just like the girls who'd been cut off from the world by their father? I was also interested in the drive to make art in a world of diminishing opportunities for creatives. The contrast between a father forcing his daughters into would-be rock stardom and Sam, who just a few generations later, is receiving the constant message to give up, felt like an interesting way to grapple with the problem. That *The Waffle Irons* persevered against peer ridicule and a possibly abusive parent to create something lasting is what keeps Sam going. She'll soon discover the irony in that, but also (I hope) a faint reason for optimism.

A question for the author

Q: What do you think makes for a good story?

A: Oh, that's tough, but with speculative fiction, I guess I would say stories that show me the future while forcing me to take a harder look at the present. My favorites often alert me to some mad, screaming deficiency in my perception. Ted Chiang's *The Great Silence* is a good example, a gut-wrenching twist on that old *Now Voyager* line, "don't let's ask for the moon. We have the stars." Or in this case, "we [still] have" these rapidly dwindling species we're paying zero attention to while we search for alien life.

About the author

Sara Kate Ellis was born in Oregon but has lived most of her adult life in Japan. She lives in Tokyo with her partner and their two ornery cats and has been served more than once by a robot bartender.

Copyright

Title information

Metaphorosis April 2022

ISSN: 2573-136X (online)
ISBN: 978-1-64076-226-8 (e-book)
ISBN: 978-1-64076-227-5 (paperback)

Publisher

Metaphorosis
a magazine of speculative fiction

Metaphorosis Magazine is an imprint of Metaphorosis Publishing
Neskowin, OR, USA

Discounts available

Substantial discounts are available for educational institutions, including writing workshops. Discounts are also available for quantity purchases. For details, contact Metaphorosis at metaphorosis.com/about

Metaphorosis Publishing

Metaphorosis offers beautifully written science fiction and fantasy. Our imprints include:

Metaphorosis Magazine
Plant Based Press
Verdage
Vestige

You can also find us:
@MetaphorosisMag, @MetaphorosisRev, @Metaphorosis
www.facebook.com/metaphorosis

Help keep Metaphorosis running by supporting us at
Patreon.com/metaphorosis

See more about some of our books on the following pages.

Metaphorosis

a magazine of speculative fiction

Metaphorosis is an online speculative fiction magazine dedicated to quality writing. We publish an original story every week, along with author bios, interviews, and notes on story origins.

We also publish monthly print and e-book issues, as well as yearly Best of and Complete anthologies.

Come and see us online at magazine.Metaphorosis.com.

Plant Based Press

plant
based
press

Vegan-friendly science fiction and fantasy, including anthologies of the year's best SFF stories, from 2016-2020.

Chambers of the Heart
speculative stories
by
B. Morris Allen

A heart that's a building, a dog that's a program, a woman sinking irretrievably — stories about love, loss, and movement.

Susurrus

A darkly romantic story of magic, love, and suffering.

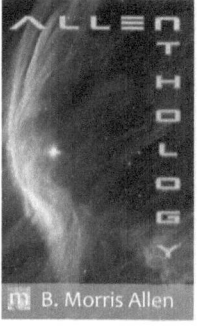

Allenthology: Volume I

Including three full collections of SFF stories.

Verdage

Science fiction and fantasy books for writers – full of great stories, often with an additional focus on the craft of speculative fiction writing.

Reading 5X5 x2

Duets

How do authors' voices change when they collaborate?

A round-robin of five talented science fiction and fantasy authors collaborating with each other and writing solo.

Including stories by Evan Marcroft, David Gallay, J. Tynan Burke, L'Erin Ogle, and Douglas Anstruther.

Score

an SFF symphony

An anthology with an emotional score from the heights of joy to the depths of despair – but always with a little hope shining through.

Reading 5X5

Five stories, five times

See how different writers take on the same material.

Reading 5X5

Writers' Edition

Two extra stories, the story seed, and authors' notes on writing.

Vestige

Novelettes, novellas, and novels by Metaphorosis authors.

The Nocturnals
Mariah Montoya

Night is Dangerous.
Day is deadly.

Where day and night last thirty years, humans move constantly stay ahead of the night and cruel Nocturnals that call it home. But a boy is lost out there.